MW01178872

Like Any Other Monday

Like Any Other Monday

A Novel by Binnie Brennan

GASPEREAU PRESS · PRINTERS & PUBLISHERS · MMXIV

CONTENTS

At the height of the vaudeville years, on any given show day, tens of thousands of performers took to the vaudeville stages working two, three, even five or more shows a day, six days a week. To these hard-working and talented men, women, and children, most of them now lost to history, I dedicate this book.

A comedian does funny things; a good comedian does things funny.   BUSTER KEATON

A Sound Like Love, 1898

A tiny boy stands in the wings, alone in the dark. Mama is on the big floor with Pop; she's picking up her horn and putting it to her mouth. Soon her music will fall from the bell. One time little Billy stood next to the horn as she played, and held out his cupped hands as though to catch the music as it fell. He never did catch it, but Mama laughed so hard she had to stop playing.

Pop is talking. Soon he will dance. The gaslight shines white-gold on his parents, making them look more perfect than they already are.

The child chews thoughtfully on a piece of bread Mama has left for him. Pop looks so grand, tall in his hat and coat, with his hands on his hips and his elbows sticking out as he speaks. Billy drops the bread and puts his hands on his hips, just like Pop. Mama's music pours into the air, and Pop begins his dance. *Hop—turn—high-kick—leap to the chair, high up on the table.* Billy hops, turns, kicks his foot in the air. Jumps onto an imaginary chair and falls back onto the floor, sitting down with a soft thump. But it doesn't hurt. It never hurts, not when you land right.

"Hey, Pop," he whispers. His father doesn't hear him; he continues his dance. All the child wants is for Pop to pick him up and throw him high in the air. He will laugh, and so will Pop, who will then throw him higher and over to the wall, where he will let Billy fall while holding onto the seat of his little trousers. He will slide to the floor and land sitting down, laughing so hard he can't breathe. This is what he wants, to play with his Pop, but he will have to wait until the lights go down and the three of them put on their coats and walk back to this week's boarding house. Once they're in their room, then Pop can throw him.

The little boy finishes the bread, and puts on his cap. Now Pop is leaping over the table. Soon he will dive over it and under it and kick his legs so high and so fast, Billy will have to watch carefully, or he will miss seeing those shiny black feet, one after another, knock the hats off the top of the coat tree.

His own feet twitch to Mama's music. Billy has an idea. Slowly he stands up and walks out into the light. Maybe no-one will see him. He is, after all, only little.

Like a miniature shadow of his father he dives low, jumps up and kicks high, then with one hand in front and one in back, he bows, sweeping the floor with his cap. Beyond the bright lights there is darkness, and from that darkness emerges a sound like love. Mama is hiding her smile behind her horn. Pop looks out at the place beyond the lights, then over at him. He winks. Then they play.

*Boffo Billy is not a midget performer, but a
revelation in eccentric juvenile talent ...*
THE NEW YORK CLIPPER, 1900

*It is a hurricane pace from start to
finish that this famous trio sets ...*
PORTLAND FAMILY THEATRE, 1900

*... the cutest atom of jollity that ever wiggled
its way into the hearts of an audience ...*
EMPIRE THEATRE, HOBOKEN, 1900

*... so unique that he follows no other infant prodigy,
and probably has no imitator on the stage ...*
AT THE ORPHEUM, 1901

*Boffo Billy Pascoe, the smallest and
funniest comedian on earth ...*
BLACK'S NEW THEATRE, 1901

*... unquestionably the funniest chap of his size ever
seen in vaudeville ... it is impossible to describe the
convulsingly funny antics of this little fellow.*
KEITH'S THEATRE, UNION SQUARE, 1902

*Little "Boffo" Billy Pascoe is said to be the most
remarkable child comedian in the world.*
AVENUE THEATRE, PITTSBURGH, 1903

CHAPTER ONE

Topper, 1916

The young man slides headfirst along the banquet table, making the most of the lame shove his father has given him. He'll gain momentum on the first forward roll, but he wishes Pop had pushed harder. A recent booze-fueled mis-kick has sprained Pop's knee and wrecked his timing, but there's no time to think about that now. Billy grits his teeth and shoots along the table, scattering plates, glasses, and cutlery as he goes. Already the audience is laughing. He tucks and rolls off the end, picks up speed and rolls twice more before tumbling over the edge of the stage and into the orchestra pit. Billy lands seated on a waiting chair next to the trombone player, who moves over to make room, still playing. With perfect timing the drummer strikes his cymbal just as the loosened legs of the chair give way and Billy lands hard, legs and arms flung high so the balcony can see what's going on. They love it.

This could be the best laugh of the night. It shouldn't be, but the gag's topper may never come. Billy thinks ahead to an alternative in case his father isn't there for him to finish this one. *Snake dance? No, the orchestra doesn't have the sheets for it. What, then?*

If he gives a solid finish, then they'll close for the rest of the week and hang on to the headline. Billy can't bear the thought of the Three Pascoes being shuffled between the dancing dogs and the monologist—or worse, opening the show. *Keep thinking, keep moving.* He hauls himself back onto the stage, rubs his head and stumbles. Puts his cap back on and waits for his father's foot to remove it: *three—two—one ...* But the kick never comes. From the corner of his eye he sees nothing, no movement, no sign of Pop coming at him.

Billy would like to hit something.

Drink has taken his father away from him, has slowed his kick, and is ruining the act. Still small for his age, Billy is now by far the stronger and steadier of the two; he is the one the audience trusts. He can coax a laugh from them with the flick of a glance, a cyclone-driven pratfall, or a gesture half-started. But Pop has lost them, is losing his son.

The kick never comes. *Where the hell is he?* Billy looks around, cowers, and recovers from nothing. He strikes a pose, fists held out before him and face set in a warning scowl. The audience murmurs in anticipation. He begins a dance of exaggerated boxing moves, alternately jabbing, cowering, and running in circles around an imagined ring, chased by an imagined opponent. The pit drummer improvises with him, delivering rim shots, whistles, and cymbal crashes. Billy jumps onto the banquet table and runs the length of it into a handspring off the end, cartwheeling hands-free downstage. He ducks, then swings his left hook hard into a spin and a flip, landing on his ass, bewildered. A swell of laughter fills the hole his father's absence has left.

Now he sees him, in the shadows of the wings, out of sight of the audience. Pop is on the floor, slumped against a packing trunk, a stage hand crouched beside him winding tape around his knee. Pop is finished for the night. He reaches for the mickey buried in his pocket. Billy narrows his eyes and then turns the gesture into a surprised blink. At times like this it's easy not to smile.

Billy pulls himself up rump-first and looks around for his invisible foe. He sees no-one, and raises his hand in victory, nodding humbly at the audience. There is a polite laugh and some clapping, but not nearly enough to close the show. If he doesn't get the boffo laugh, they'll lose the headline, and he'll be damned if they're forced to open the rest of the week. Billy puffs out his chest, raises both arms and waves, turning as though to strut offstage. Without warning, his legs shoot out from under him and he falls backward, up onto his shoulder and into a kicking spin that goes on longer than any pratfall he has ever done. He spins and turns again and again, everything around him a blur, even the sound of the audience's love.

Long before he lands, Billy knows two things. He knows by the shouts of laughter that he has topped the orchestra pit gag. And he knows too that this is the last fall he will do as one of the Three Pascoes.

Billy Pascoe picks himself up, faces the crowd, and offers them a simple bow. To the sound of their shouts and whistles he exits stage-left, striding through the wings past his father and out the stage door into the cold November night.

*

"Where ya think you're going?"

Billy pauses with one hand on the trunk, ready to slam it shut. The air in the room is tight, and he can't seem to unclench his jaw. The backs of his legs are still quivering from his sprint to the hotel.

He looks at his mother, standing in the doorway clutching her saxophone, knuckles white against the black case. She seems smaller than usual in her wool coat, her face dulled by fatigue and resignation.

"God help me, Ma, I can't take it anymore. Neither can you." His voice emerges rough and husky, lower than usual.

There is a long silence while Myra stares at him, her dark eyes sunk into carved cheekbones. Once she was pretty; now she is worn-down, gaunt. This is how she will look as an old woman, Billy thinks as he lowers the lid to the packing trunk and closes the latch. He glances at the second of three trunks.

"I'm taking these two down to the station. You and I'll go back to Muskoka and figure something out. Give me your horn and I'll pack it."

Myra looks over at her husband's trunk, which stands in the corner of the room. Everything Joe needs is in there, right down to the three bourbon bottles he's stashed. She closes her eyes and nods, holds out the saxophone to her son.

*

The Pullman was his first rocker. From childhood Billy has taken comfort in its rhythm, the smell of its steam, the sound of its whistle and the clatter of its wheels. Until recently, train journeys have brought him a sense of thrill and adventure as the Three Pascoes moved by rail from one city to the next, the welcoming roar of a theatre audience awaiting their entrance, the luxury of two shows per day. Old friends reunited backstage, laughing and shaking hands, slapping each others' backs.

Lately, though, the train journeys have filled Billy with boredom and dread, wondering if his and his father's bruises will heal enough during their travel day to withstand three punishing shows a day, six days a week; if his father will lay off the drink for a while. Praying he can stand one more week of trading on-stage with Pop, real fights conducted under the cover of comedy.

In the seat across from him, Myra's head nods in rhythm to the train's steady lurch. Tomorrow they will move to a sleeper car; with their tickets bought in haste, they were lucky to board today's eastbound train at all. Billy reaches for the travel rug in the overhead rack and tucks it around his mother's shoulders, then sits back in his seat and stares out the window at the darkness. Muskoka is days away from Vancouver; sooner or later he will give in to sleep.

It is dark, nearly midnight. No doubt Pop is still at the saloon. Soon enough he'll return to the hotel, stumble up the stairs and find their door unlocked, his packing trunk standing alone in the room. He'll pull out a bottle and load himself up some more, and then pass out sprawled across the bed.

Billy wonders if anything will ease the knot that's been lodged in his gut for so long he's lost count—weeks, months, maybe even years. He reaches up to switch off the reading lamp and looks out at the night sky, the snow-lit mountains. The rocking of the Pullman invites him. He fights the urge to close his eyes.

CHAPTER TWO

Lakeshore

Billy shoves the packing trunks between the sawhorses and releases the tabletop from the hooks on the wall. The salt shaker knocks against his head; he bats it out of the way and steps back, watching the salt and pepper dance like puppets on strings tacked to the ceiling. Ma always gets a kick out of things like that, dangling pieces of whimsy that have their use. Every summer, Billy figures out some crazy invention to make her laugh.

Already Myra has filled her pipe and gone off to find a pinochle game. There are enough old-timers around now staying through winter at the Lakeshore Actors' Colony that they'll keep each other company—and who knows, warm, probably—until the troupers return late spring, ready for their summer layoff.

The mattresses need airing, and later on Billy will take the blankets outside to get rid of the mothballs and shake out the mouse dirt. But first he wants to check on the boats. He pushes the screen door open and pauses before the porch, breathing deeply of the crisp, piney air. The cottage smells wrong in the cold, and the mid-afternoon light slanting across the floor is at a different angle from summer light. But beyond the porch and down the hill, the lake is its usual glassy, grey perfection. Maybe later he'll take a dip, let the cold wake him up.

The grass crunches underfoot as Billy jogs toward the boathouse. He takes a quick turn around the sand lot; a puddle in the groove by home plate holds a membrane of ice with water trapped underneath. Billy swings an invisible bat, spins around twice, and stops short of taking a pratfall. Instead he places a toe on the ice and watches it crack beneath his foot.

The boathouse door creaks opens, letting in a flood of light. Water slaps against hulls and the musky tang of varnish and canvas nearly overwhelms him. Billy walks around slowly, checking and tightening the painter lines, reading the names of the boats: *Dixie Pirate*, *Elk*, and *Damfino*. Old friends, elegant wooden vessels whose striped canopies have shaded countless waterside parties, women dressed in long white skirts and short sleeves, children trailing their hands in the waves, the men tanned, handsome, and laughing, always laughing.

A swell from the lake lifts the boats and sets the bumpers creaking against the dock. At the far end of the boathouse, up on the deck, three rowboats and a small sailboat sit belly up, dry for the winter. More painted names, *Minnow*, *Guppy*, *Kingfisher*, and lastly, named for him, *Boffo*. Billy runs a hand over the lettering. "Boffo Billy, Prince of Vaudeville": Pop could never let a headline like that one go. The little white sloop was his fifteenth birthday present, following the Pascoes' most lucrative season. Billy had spent most of his waking hours that summer catching the breeze and slicing through water, and when he wasn't aboard *Boffo*, he was sanding and painting and making mechanical adjustments to her. Rolled up in a duffel bag underneath is her sail, a bright blue canvas. He hadn't had time to check the stitching before closing up for the season. It's been bothering him since they left for the circuit in September. Billy hates unfinished business.

*

"Pikey says come on over for some perch later on, he'll fry you up a plate."

Billy looks up from the sail in his hands.

"The Perch Hut's open this time of year?"

Myra drags on her pipe, blows a ring into the air.

"Yep, seems there's enough of us still around to give him some business. He'll stay through until mid-December, then he and Stella head down to Toronto to stay with the kids for Christmas. Says he's got a special perch for you; he knows how much you like it."

"Who else is around?" Billy asks.

"Sam Curtis is here. Jimmy McCasson's widow, Thelma and her sister. The Bellmans have sent their kids off to work the circuit on their own this year. Sally figures she and Pete have earned their time off; besides, Pete's leg gave out last time he was on stage. Never been right since he fell off the wire that time in Baltimore. We've got a pinochle game going that'll keep him off his feet." Myra reaches out a hand across the table. "Here, give me that. And let me have some light."

Billy moves the oil lamp closer to her and hands over the sail. He picks up a deck of cards and lays out a game of solitaire while he watches his mother deftly weave the needle and thread in and out around the edge.

"Know who else is here?" she says without raising her eyes, "Norma and Lucinda Hart."

Billy shakes his head in disbelief.

"The Hart Sisters? But they're my age. Why aren't they out trouping? Last I saw them was in Calgary, I think, in March. They were closing the first half, doing great. Audience loved 'em."

"Yeah, well. Seems somebody loved one of 'em, anyways. Norma's in the family way. Too far along to get rid of the baby, so she'll wait it out here. Billy, you're blushing!"

"But she's only ..."

"She's old enough to know better. No matter, it can't be helped."

Billy thinks of the two girls, slim and delicate in satin dresses, singing parlour songs and dancing in toe shoes.

"What'll they do for money?" he asks.

"Good question. Let's hope the father'll do right by her. She won't marry him, but maybe he'll see fit to set her up, leastways until she's back on her feet." The thread catches, and Myra gives it a tug. "She's strong-willed, that Norma is. Had to be since their parents died; she's been both mother and father to Lucinda."

"How'd their parents die?"

"Tuberculosis, one right after another. It was a terrible time. I suppose Norma was sixteen, Lucinda twelve or thirteen years old. We all took up a collection to help pay for the funerals. Pop and a few others saw to it that the girls kept working, helped them re-book themselves as a sister act."

Billy reaches for more wood and throws it in the stove. He looks at his mother, her head bent over the sail, punching the needle in, out, and through the canvas. There's a long winter ahead; he can't avoid the question of money.

"I'm thinking up some gags for a single act," he says. "I'll go back on the road in a few weeks, but I need to figure out a way to do it."

"How're you gonna do that with no-one to play off of?" Myra asks. She knots the thread and puts it between her teeth.

It's a question he's been asking himself as he thinks through gags he knows he'll never top on his own.

"I'll figure something out," he says quietly.

"Meanwhile, you can let some of your bumps and bruises heal," she says. "And maybe ..."

Billy looks up from his solitaire game.

"Maybe Joe can heal up some, too."

She looks away into the shadows of the cottage, alone with her thoughts. Billy lays down his cards. Suddenly he's ready for some perch. He stands and pulls on his coat, and reaches for the door. Surely old Pike's got a cold beer for him to wash it down with.

CHAPTER THREE

Broom

Billy steps inside the clubhouse dining hall and looks around. Sunlight filters through cracks in the shutters and spills across the rows of tables. Billy pulls open one indoor shutter, then another, letting in enough light to reveal a thin layer of dust on the stage floor, enough to slip him up if he lands wrong. In the galley he finds a broom; soon he has swept a neat pile of dust off to the side of the stage.

"They always said you could do everything with a broom but sweep."

From the corner of his eye, Billy spots Norma standing in the doorway. Without skipping a beat, he upends the broomstick and starts giving traffic signals with it, stopping invisible cars going in one direction while waving others through. Then he fumbles with the broom handle and fakes tripping over it and lands in a pratfall, facing away from her. He is not ready to look at her just yet.

"Billy. I won't bite." Her voice comes from just beyond the stage. He sits up and sees her silhouetted against the sunlit window.

"Norma," he says. His cap has fallen on the floor, close enough for him to hook it with the broom handle. He flips it into the air and aims his head underneath. Misses.

"It's good to see you, Billy. A bit of a surprise, though."

Norma places her hands on the apron of the stage. Billy

grabs his cap and scoots over, holds out his hand and helps her up. Even pregnant, she is light as a feather. But she is without question pregnant, with a swelling the size of a basketball ill-concealed beneath her skirt. They sit side-by-side, legs dangling. Billy opens his mouth to speak, but can't think what to say.

"I know," she says, as though reading his thoughts, "You're surprised to see me, too. Your mother has been very kind, you know. She's offered to stay until ..." As Norma glances downward, Billy feels a flush creeping up his neck.

"Is he taking care of you?" he asks. "I mean, has he given you ..."

"He's given me enough, thanks," Norma says. For the first time, Billy looks at her, takes in her enormous, pale eyes which completely dominate her heart-shaped face. She would resemble a china doll, were it not for the shadows beneath her eyes, the grim set to her jaw.

"I can take care of myself," she says. "It's Lucinda I'm worried about. She wants to go back on the circuit, put away some money. What about you, Billy?"

"What do you mean?" he asks.

"Your mother told me you've broken up the act. What'll you do next?"

"I'm working on some gags, thinking of going solo for the rest of the season."

There is a question in her eyes, one he doesn't want to hear.

"How's that going to work?"

Billy squirms, fiddles with the brim of his cap. It's not working; it'll never work. He can't improvise gags against himself, not for seventeen minutes, three times a day, six days a week.

"Billy, I have an idea."

"Oh, no you don't," he mutters.

"Billy, yes. Please listen to me. Won't you consider working something up with Lu? She's a hard worker, a good dancer. Sings like a nightingale. Surely you two could ..."

"Norma, I ..." Once again the words fail him.

Norma puts her hand on his wrist and turns to face him. "Oh, Billy, please! Won't you just give it a chance?"

"But ... I don't ..."

"Billy. Tell me what choice you have, what choice she has. Please, Billy?"

Norma's eyes fill with tears. If only her lip wouldn't quiver; he prays it won't.

It does.

CHAPTER FOUR

Singing Class

"Take your uke," Myra says without looking up from her solitaire game.

Billy shakes his head and stuffs his slap-shoes into his rucksack.

"What do I want that for?" he says.

"She sings, don't she? Go on, take it. Might come in handy."

"She sings parlour songs. I play parody." Billy rolls up some extra felt padding and puts it in with his shoes. He may not need his ukulele, but if he's going to show Lucinda how to fall, she'll need some padding. His mother looks up at him, her brow furrowed in exasperation.

"Well, then, it's perfect. Let her sing straight and you do your parody. Take your uke."

Myra's right. Why didn't he think of it? He drags out his trunk and fishes around for his ukulele, strums a few chords and winces. Turns a peg until it slips into tune, hopes it'll stay there during the cold walk to the clubhouse.

"Got any other ideas?" he asks. Myra's spent her entire life on the stage; she's done it all. From her daddy's medicine show act through the Two Pascoes' early years in vaudeville playing five-a-day, until Billy joined the act as a kid and they graduated to three-a-day, and finally the Big Time, two-a-day, Myra Pascoe has sung, danced, played straight, played funny, played her saxophone, and given her opinion on just about every act they've ever seen. Her instinct for what works is infallible, her comic timing impeccable. Billy watches as she lays down her last card. She puffs on her pipe and squints at him through the smoke.

"Find out what she can do. Then do it funny." Myra picks up the deck of cards, smacks it against the table, and shuffles. Lays out another hand.

*

He hears her before he sees her. Over the clanging of the piano, Lucinda's voice flips up and down a series of arpeggios, low, then high, then low again. The off-key piano chords move up by half-steps and her voice follows, until he thinks surely there are no more high notes to be reached, but she keeps going. Soundlessly, he takes the stairs by twos and stops outside the dining hall doorway. Finally she's reached her limit, and the ringing of her last note fades.

Billy shifts his rucksack to the other shoulder and steps into the room. The two sisters turn to look at him, Norma seated at the piano and Lucinda standing off to one side of her. Lucinda is taller than he remembers from the last time he saw her, slim and graceful, her black hair pulled back.

"Billy," Norma calls out as he moves between the tables to the stage. "You remember Lu."

Lucinda nods; he nods back. Her face is young, an echo of her sister's with her pale blue eyes, but rounder and lacking Norma's guardedness. She's just a kid, he thinks.

"The piano needs help," Norma says. "It sounds like it's just been dragged in from a saloon."

She plays a few chords and the dissonance jangles the air. Billy pulls his ukulele from the rucksack and strums a few chords. There's no use waiting; he might as well start.

"You know *The Moonshiner*?" he says, and starts playing. Lucinda's eyes widen and she looks nervously at her sister. Billy hums a few bars, sings a verse. Norma nods and joins in on the piano. By the end of the verse she's got it. Now Lucinda's humming; soon she joins the chorus, blushing pink at the words and singing quietly.

"Wait," Norma says, stopping them with a slap to the piano keys. "What if Lu sings *When Flowers Bloom in Springtime* while you sing this? I think we can make the chords work. We heard Roberts and Cole do it once, remember, Lu?"

Lucinda nods, opens her mouth and sings. For a moment Billy listens to the ache of her voice as it reaches around the old parlour melody and pulls a story out of the air. Norma follows, searching quietly with her fingers flying across the piano keys until suddenly her eyes widen and she nods him in. Billy hops up and seats himself on the piano top with his legs crossed at the knees and starts strumming *The Moonshiner*. He throws his head back and brays, sending the raunchy words bounding around the room while Lucinda stands poised, clasping her hands before her and singing like a nightingale, her voice soaring above his baritone.

Norma looks up from the keyboard and shakes her head, laughing. Billy winks and belts out another verse.

Find out what she can do, his mother had said. *Then do it funny.*

This may work after all.

CHAPTER FIVE

Ballet Class

"I'll write up a lead-sheet for you to take on the road."
Norma scribbles some notes on the back of a song sheet.
"Just hand it to the pianist and make sure he starts in
B-flat." She finishes writing and smiles expectantly at
Lucinda, then Billy. "What'll you do next?"

Billy looks at Lucinda, who is staring at her feet. There
is a long pause, during which Billy wonders not for the first
time what he's gotten himself into.

"Maybe we should see if someone will write us a script,"
she finally says.

"Uh-uh, no scripts," Billy says.

"It's a good idea, Billy," Norma says. "If you're doing
a Two-act, you'll need a script. How will you fill fifteen
minutes?"

"I've never worked from a script," he says. "Never need-
ed it. We can find our own material. The dueling song's a
good start. Lu, you can dance, can't you? I can get into all
sorts of trouble around your dancing. Tie up your shoes and
we'll try something."

Lucinda frowns, looks at her sister. Norma hands over
her satin slippers and nods.

"Try it, Lu. Let's see what happens."

While Lucinda winds the ribbons around her ankles,

Billy shakes the grit from the soles of his slap-shoes and laces them up.

"I haven't danced in a few weeks," she says. "I should probably warm up first."

She hops down from the stage, rests a hand on the edge, and begins to stretch, first moving her arm in an arc over her head. Billy leans forward and grasps his ankles in his hands, then begins a calisthenics set. All the while he is thinking, wondering how he can play off a ballerina. From time to time he glances over at Lucinda, then at Norma, who is playing a classical piano piece, maybe Mozart.

He is on the floor of the stage doing push-ups when he looks up and sees the broom leaning against the wall. Lucinda has one leg stretched before her, her foot resting on the lip of the stage as it would a barre. Billy looks from the foot to the broom and back again. He closes his eyes, and in that instant the scenario starts to unfold in his mind. He jumps to his feet.

"I got it!" he shouts, and Norma stops playing and Lucinda's head whips up from her knee, their two sets of blue eyes on him.

"Lu, keep stretching," he calls out, and he grabs the broom and hops down to the floor beside her. "Norma, keep playing. We're in ballet class."

Billy steps back a few paces and lets them start. While Norma plays and Lucinda stretches, he sweeps the floor, seemingly unaware of Lucinda. He sweeps here and there, pauses to inspect something invisible on the floor, turns the broom over and taps the invisible something with the handle. He resumes sweeping, lifts an imaginary rug and brushes his dust pile underneath. Looks around to make sure nobody is watching. Spots Lucinda and is instantly smitten.

"Ignore me, Lu," he calls out, "Pretend I'm not here."

Lucinda switches from stretching to pliés while Billy clasps his hands together and makes doe-eyes at her. He walks up behind her and watches with interest as she rises from a plié. Up and down she goes, Billy's head following. He leans the broom against the stage and places his hand on the edge, and imitates her, once, twice. The third time he is stuck with his knees bent.

"Keep playing, Norma. You don't see me either," he calls out.

While Lucinda rises and falls with grace, Billy struggles to stand up, mops his brow and topples to the floor, taking the broom with him, sending his cap skittering. He grabs the broom and crawls after his cap, and clambers to his feet.

"Okay, look at me now, Lu."

"How?" she asks, as she looks his way.

"Like I'm a dolt," he says, and as he doffs his cap with his eyes wide and shy, Lucinda purses her lips, shakes her head, and looks back at the imaginary barre.

Billy looks momentarily stricken, then hopeful. He crosses his arms in satisfaction. The broom handle catches him by the ankles and he collapses in a pratfall.

*

"Well?" Billy looks first at Lucinda, then at Norma. Norma is nodding her head slowly. "I think it's funny," she says.

The word hangs in the air until once again Lucinda purses her lips and shakes her head.

[37]

"How is it funny?" she asks. A frown cuts into her smooth brow. Norma eases herself from the piano bench and smiles.

"Oh, it's funny, Lu. You're playing straight to Billy's comedy. It's perfect."

"But what's funny about it? All he's doing is falling over and making a ... a fool of himself."

"What do you think comedy is, Lu?" Billy asks.

"Well, that's just the point." Lucinda's voice is rising. "I don't know what comedy is, so how can you expect me to know how to perform it? Oh, this will never work!" She blinks twice and her lower lip twitches.

Don't cry, Billy thinks. *Oh god, please don't cry.* He turns his head so he won't have to see the tears spilling down her cheeks. When he looks again she is gone, the sound of her light footsteps subsiding on the wooden stairs.

Billy rubs a hand across his forehead and looks at Norma.

"You know when there's a Chinese act on the bill?" he asks. "And they do the greatest, most beautiful work onstage, and then afterward when you try to congratulate them, they start talking to you in crazy sounding words that make no sense?"

"I think comedy scares her, Billy. She doesn't understand it. Doesn't trust herself to be funny."

"But she doesn't have to try to be funny if she's playing straight," Billy says, "I'll do the work. The less she does, the easier it is for me."

"You know that, and I know that. Try telling her next time you see her. Meanwhile, give me a list of your songs and I'll try to match another one up with one of ours."

Norma hands Billy her song sheet and a pencil. He licks the lead and stares at the empty page.

[38]

"It's a good idea, the ballet class," she says. "Where did it come from?"

Billy taps his head with the pencil and starts writing. Norma's right, it is a good idea. The gag possibilities are endless.

"I think it'll get a lot of laughs." She bites her lip. "You know, we rehearse a lot. Lucinda needs to make sure she knows what it all feels like and how it's going to run. I'm the same way. Ad libbing is scary if you're not used to it."

CHAPTER SIX

Comedy Class

His mother is sitting on a camp chair on the porch, wrapped in a shawl and facing the lake with her eyes closed. Fallen leaves drift around her feet.

"How's the view in there?" he asks as he lowers his rucksack to the floor.

"It'll do," she replies, keeping her eyes closed. "You find any material?"

"I got a few ideas. Some of 'em may work."

"Anything involve your uke?"

"Yes, Ma. Norma's working on a duet for us to sing."

"Pretty voice, as I recall," Myra says. Her eyes are still firmly shut.

"Yeah," Billy says. "Yeah ..."

"But?" Myra snaps her eyes open. She never misses a trick, always knows when something's bothering him. Billy sits on the step and looks out over the lake.

"Lucinda's afraid of comedy. She wants a script, wants to rehearse everything."

"She's a singer, a dancer," Myra says, "That's how they do it."

"But she doesn't even understand comedy, she said so herself. Then she cried and left."

"Well then, it sounds as though she's halfway there."

"What do you mean?"

"Comedy is just a half-step over from tragedy," Myra says, closing her eyes once more to let the words sink in.

"Pop and I, we never had to talk about it. We just did it."

"You and your father knew each other's ways. You knew what worked and you trusted each other ..."

She looks at her lap and leaves the words unfinished. Billy twists the leather rucksack strap between his thumb and forefinger.

"Speaking of Pop." From beneath the shawl she produces a yellow telegram. Billy's heart speeds up as he looks at it.

"What is it?" he says. "Is Pop coming home? Wait, is he ..."

"There's no black border, he's fine. Go on, read it."

Billy shakes his head. "Just tell me, Ma."

Myra sighs, looks at him, then looks at the telegram.

"He won't be coming home any time soon," she says, and then draws a sharp breath. "Your Pop's in jail, Billy. He broke some poor fellow's jaw in a bar-room fight with a hitch kick and now he's got to do six months. He made it as far as the border, the silly ass, before he was caught."

Billy gives the strap a hard twist as a complicated mix of fury tempered with relief tightens the knot in his stomach.

"What'd he have to go and do that for," he says.

"Better some stranger than you on-stage again," Myra says. "Remember the time he got you in the back of the head, knocked you out for eighteen hours? And he was stone-cold sober. Only ever happened the once, thank the lord."

Billy shuts his eyes at the memory.

"Maybe he'll dry out in jail," he says.

For a long moment they sit together, Myra with her

eyes closed and Billy staring at the water, trying hard not to remember his father's lean and wary face, the sound of his voice. But it doesn't work. It never works. Billy can no more rinse Pop from his thoughts than he can wash away his own fingerprints.

Eventually, Myra stands up from the chair and looks down at him.

"Well, there's more than one way to skin a cat," she says. "Your entire life you've been doing things one way. You and that girl, you'll find your comedy."

CHAPTER SEVEN

Sisters

"I knew I'd find you here."

Lucinda shifts on the bench to make room for her sister. "I brought a picnic. And a blanket."

Norma sits and spreads the blanket over their laps. She pulls two apples from her coat pocket and holds one out to Lucinda.

"Hungry?" she asks, as she takes a bite out of her apple.

Lucinda shakes her head. Nothing could be further from her thoughts than eating; her stomach is clenched from nerves, and it feels as though there's a bird flapping around in her chest. For a while they sit companionably with nothing but the sound of waves lapping the shore and the crunching of Norma's apple to interrupt their thoughts.

"Soon the lake's going to freeze," Norma finally says.

Lucinda nods and thinks if it weren't for the trees on the distant shore, the line between the pearl-grey sky and the surface of the lake would be indiscernible. And if Norma hadn't gone and gotten pregnant, Lucinda wouldn't need to work to support the two of them—soon three. And she wouldn't be near paralyzed with fright at the thought of performing something so new, so foreign, with a total stranger. All of this she thinks about as she sits on the bench, looking out over the water.

"He thinks you're good, Lu," Norma says in a quiet voice.

"I can't imagine how that's possible," Lucinda says, shaking her head.

"You did what he asked you to do, and it was funny. He even said it was funny."

Lucinda's throat tightens and she swallows back the threat of tears.

"I don't know the first thing about comedy," she finally says. "So how can I perform it? And without a script? There's no earthly way I can do it."

Norma takes her cold hand in her own.

"You can *be* funny without doing anything funny," she says. "Let him come up with the gags, Lu. See where he takes you."

"You'd be so much better at this, Norma," Lucinda says. Her nose has started to run. "You're fearless, you'll try anything."

Norma breathes a small laugh and looks down at her belly.

"I don't mean ... You know what I mean," Lucinda says.

"You're as brave as anyone I know, Lu. You have a more beautiful singing voice, and you're a much better dancer than I am." Norma holds out a corner of the blanket and dabs Lucinda's nose with it. "Who knows, maybe it's just as well you don't understand what's funny and what isn't; it'll make a better straight-man out of you. There, now, don't cry."

Lucinda rests her head on her sister's shoulder and breathes the tang of mothballs drifting from the blanket on their laps.

"Remember the first time we saw the Three Pascoes?" Norma says. "It was at Loewe's Theatre in Ottawa. Joe

Pascoe was reciting a poem and Billy was getting into trouble with the broom, pounding away at an invisible bug on the floor. He must have been twelve years old at the time."

Norma tightens her arm around Lucinda's shoulders.

"That broom went clear through a knothole in the floor, and Billy landed on his head with his legs up in the air. They had more fun trying to pull that broom out of the hole in the floor. Remember what happened when they finally did? The handle was covered in bright yellow mustard."

In spite of herself, Lucinda smiles.

"Someone told me that it was the Three Leightons who did that," Norma continues. "They hid below-stage and painted mustard all over it."

Norma nudges her until the two of them are giggling, just like they used to do all the time.

"Billy made up that gag on the spot," Norma says. "It's how he works best. He's Boffo Billy, the funniest boy in vaudeville. We're lucky he's willing to try this; it's a great opportunity. You can do it, Lu," she says gently. "You can be his straight partner. He can't do it without you."

Lucinda squeezes her sister's hand, tries to ignore the nervous fluttering in her chest.

"You think so?" she asks.

"I can see the bill: 'Pascoe & Hart: Vaudeville's Funniest Two-act.' Can't you just hear the applause?"

Lucinda breathes deeply. "I'll try, Norma," she says. "And I'll apologize to Billy for running out of the rehearsal. That was unprofessional of me."

Norma holds out the second apple. "Coming home?" she asks.

"No, I think I'll stay here awhile," Lucinda says.

"I'll leave the blanket with you, then." Norma leans over and kisses her cheek, then she stands slowly and makes her way along the shoreline toward their cabin. She pauses to pick up a few sticks of driftwood for the fireplace, straightens, and makes her way along the footpath and into a stand of pine trees. Even this far along Norma moves with grace and certainty. *Who's the better dancer,* Lucinda asks herself as she polishes the apple on the blanket and bites into its crisp, shiny skin.

CHAPTER EIGHT

Diving

From the roof of the boathouse Billy looks out over the lake, beyond the rocky outcrop known as Deadman's Jut, where he and his buddy Lex like to take girls for a picnic by boat. Last summer they enticed two Russian contortionists named Serafina and Petra, who had stopped by the colony to visit a distant aunt after a week's run at the Gravenhurst Opera House. Contortionists, Lex had proclaimed, would bring new thrills to their limited sexual experience. What they hadn't anticipated was the girls' complete lack of interest in them. It wasn't simply a question of language; after eating the sandwiches Lex had prepared, and having drunk most of the whiskey Billy had pilfered from his father's supply, the girls spent the rest of the afternoon ignoring them, stretching each others' legs over their heads front and back, and giggling and whispering to each other. The stretching act had just about killed Billy, but it was the girls' falling asleep in each others' arms, curled against the base of the Jut's one scrawny tree that did him in. Lex had coped with their failure by slipping into the lake and swimming back to the shore, leaving Billy with the sailboat and two sleeping, but utterly remote, beauties.

Dark clouds hang over the distant trees and a curl of smoke threads the sky beyond the Jut, likely from a year-rounder's cabin in the woods on the opposite shore. Billy pulls off his shirt, unbuttons the fly of his trousers, and stands shivering in his underwear. It wouldn't be his first time diving off the boathouse roof by any stretch, but it'll be his first dive outside the summer months. It was his father who showed him how to dive, as he had shown him just about everything else that mattered—how to take a pratfall, what to do when there's a fire in the hotel. How to knock the hat off a fellow's head with a hitch kick. Or break his jaw.

His breath comes in shallow drags as he looks at the water below, calm and inviting, deceptive in the late-November chill. In a swift motion Billy yanks off his under-shirt and steps out of his shorts, raises his arms over his head and pushes off from the roof.

It's as though a bomb has gone off in his head as he crash-es through the ice-water's surface. For a moment he lies suspended, the pain of searing cold knocking the sense from him. Then he moves his arms and begins to kick, pulling himself with powerful strokes along the bottom of the lake, ignoring the scraping of rocks and rotting branches against his chest. His lungs ache, and as he looks up to the beckon-ing ripples of sky-light, he opens his mouth in an underwa-ter roar that carries him, screaming, to break through to the air. His voice shatters the stillness of the lake, and he looks back, spluttering, at the boathouse. Already his arms are stiffening with the cold. He begins the swim back to land.

With numbed fingers he hauls himself naked and gasp-ing onto the dock, his limbs palsied with cold and a mantle of icy water pouring off him. He crawls through the door and inside the boathouse, and it's only when he grasps one slippery hand with the other and pulls his knees to his chest that he allows the tears to come, burning a trail along the hollows of his frozen cheeks. He opens his mouth and his sobs ring through the boathouse. Half frozen, at last Billy feels something.

*

Lucinda nibbles around the apple core, pleased and a bit surprised that her appetite has returned. Since the girls left the circuit she's been eating like a bird, unlike Norma, whose appetite has been voracious. Never has Lucinda seen her eat so much in one sitting, sometimes two bowls of beans and half a loaf of bread. Eating for two, Norma tells her. It's just as well Lucinda hasn't been hungry, what with the dwindling amount of cash in her grouch bag.

Norma's right. Billy is giving them a great opportunity. She will try, she really will try to be funny, and follow his lead. Billy has the best comic timing in vaudeville; for years the theatre managers have fallen all over each other to book the Three Pascoes with Billy as headliner. At least they had done, until recently. The story of Joe Pascoe's temper made the rounds practically before he'd finished chasing Mr. Black out of his own theatre, screaming blue murder through the streets of New York until Mr. Black dashed into the police station. Sure, he's a difficult man with a mean streak, but the last thing any act wants to do is annoy a theatre manager. Joe Pascoe should have known better.

Lucinda tosses the apple core into the water, watches it bob and then float toward the sandy shore where leaves lie softened and browned at the water's edge. She stands, stretches, and folds the blanket, then begins the walk along the beach. It's peaceful here, so quiet and lovely, but soon the snow will come and it'll be too cold to stay here. She can't imagine Norma and Mrs. Pascoe surviving winter in their little cabins without plumbing and electricity. Perhaps someone in town can take them in; surely there's a rooming house in Gravenhurst that'll be looking for winter tenants.

The quiet is suddenly broken by a cannonball crash in the water. Lucinda stops and turns in the direction of the sound, toward the docks by the boathouse. She scans the water's surface and sees only a slight ripple. A finger of dread prods her as she catches sight of a pair of dark trousers sliding off the roof of the boathouse. In the same instant she starts running, a howl emerges from the lake and she sees him bursting to the surface.

"Billy?" she calls. *Why is he swimming, it's too cold to swim.* "Billy!" she screams his name again and again as she sprints toward the docks. She darts through the stand of pines, brushing aside twigs and branches, tripping on tree roots, propelled by the terror of what she might find when she arrives at the boathouse. *Don't let him drown, please don't let him drown.*

When finally she sets foot on the wooden dock she stops short. He has beaten her to it; he's not drowned. But the sound coming from inside the boathouse is unlike anything she's ever heard, the uncontrolled sobbing of a grown man. Lucinda is still somehow holding on to the blanket; she clutches it to her chest and with a shaking hand she pushes the door open.

Billy is sitting on the floor curled like a baby, his head bent over his knees and his body convulsed with tremors. His nakedness shocks the breath from her and for a moment she closes her eyes against the sight of him. When

[52]

she looks again his head is turned facing her. It's too late to run.

"H-how long ... you been s-standing ..." The words trip through his chattering teeth as he glares at her, his eyes brilliant with the cold and his tears.

Every muscle on him is ropey, taut, covered in twitching gooseflesh. Lucinda forces her feet forward, moving toward him in careful steps. She drapes the blanket across his shoulders and as she rubs some warmth into his back, the chill reaches through to the palms of her hands.

"Come on, Billy, you'll freeze to death," Lucinda says, trying to keep her voice even. She places a hand under his elbow and tries to help him to his feet. He makes it partway, and then sits down hard.

"I can't," he croaks. "N-not yet."

The shoulder beneath her hand begins to heave and as she crouches beside him and wraps her arms around him, he leans into her and sobs hot, choking tears.

CHAPTER NINE

Barre Practice

Billy takes a few more turns with the screwdriver and sets the second stand on the floor, jiggling it to make sure it's level.

"What're you tinkering with, now?" Myra asks.

"I'm trying to make a dance practice barre we can take on the road, something I can take apart and carry," Billy says.

He sets the two stands about six feet apart and lays a piece of thick dowelling across them, clamping it in place. He grasps the dowelling and puts some weight on it, lifts his foot onto it and bounces. One of the stands jiggles across the porch and the dowelling clatters to the floor.

"Damn," he mutters. "It needs to carry most of my weight without slipping."

"How about some rubber matting underneath it?" Myra asks, "Just like the padding your father nailed to the feet of the table to keep it from going all over the stage while you two were jumping on it. Have a look in the kitchen cupboard, I think he kept some there."

Billy traces the foot of a stand around the rubber matting, cuts it out and hammers it in place, then he does the same for the other stand. He puts the dowelling across and tests it again and it doesn't budge.

"Perfect," he says. "Now I've got to write up a one-sheet."

"You leave that to me and get on over to the dining hall

with that contraption. I'll bring it over later and have a look at what you two are up to."

Billy leans down and gives his mother a quick kiss on the cheek. This is beginning to feel like old times, the excitement of a new show, a new season. He has been brimming with gag ideas, and last night was no exception: six times he got up in the night and stepped out onto the porch, shivering, as he made notes by the light of the moon. He can't wait to try them out with Lucinda.

"Thanks, Ma. Norma and Lu should be there already," he says, "Norma's got a new song for us to try out. Lu likes to warm up."

"Go on, then," Myra says, "Don't keep them waiting."

Billy takes the barre apart and tucks the pieces under his arm.

"Here's your slap-shoes."

Myra laces them together and drapes them over his shoulder, and he lopes off toward the yacht club.

*

"I haven't used a real barre in ages," Lucinda says. "Will it hold?"

"Give it a try," Billy says.

Lucinda puts her hand on the barre and leans on it. Billy watches closely as she bends forward and sweeps her free hand above her head, kicking her left leg behind her, and does it again. The barre stays put. And Billy has an idea.

"Can you do that again?" he asks, and as she sweeps her arm forward and kicks her leg back, a gag takes shape in his mind.

[56]

"Billy, you've got that look in your eye," Norma says from her seat at the piano.

"Let's try something," he says, moving into position. "Norma, you got something quiet in four? Lu, ignore me. I want to line up your hand with my nose."

Billy puts his hands on his hips and watches with interest as Lucinda reaches forward, then kicks back. He steps in closer, and while watching her foot, she taps his nose with the back of her hand.

"That's it," he says. "Now, do it again, then give me time to step back so you can kick me in the trousers. One-two-three-four ..."

Norma plays a soft march on the piano as Lucinda reaches forward, kicks back, and Billy watches her foot. He steps in for a closer look and she sweeps her hand forward, connecting with his nose. Billy clutches his face and staggers backward just as Lucinda's foot swings back. Her foot misses.

"Almost," Billy says. "I need to take one more step back. Maybe you can kick just a little bit higher, Lu."

"All right, but I don't want to hurt you," she says.

Billy looks over at Norma, and the two of them snort with laughter.

"My father's been kicking my ass since I was a baby," Billy says. "Give me all you've got."

Lucinda's eyes widen at his cuss word, but she nods her head.

"All right, I'll try," she says. "Let's do it again."

"On four," Billy says, and again he counts them in. Her hand swipes his nose, Billy staggers back clutching his face, and her leg swings back perfectly, landing a kick to the seat of his trousers. Billy jumps forward, clutching his behind with a startled expression on his deadpan face, and shoots her a mock-dirty look.

"Perfect!" he says. "Nice kick, Lu. How'd it look to you, Norma?"

"If that doesn't get you a belly laugh, I don't know what will," Norma says. "Why not ask the drummer to give you a smack on the high hat when Lucinda gets you in the nose, then the bass drum when she kicks you?"

"Good idea," Billy says.

"You sure that didn't hurt?" Lucinda asks.

"It doesn't hurt if I'm ready for it," Billy says. "You can go even harder. We'll call it the back-kick, and I'll whisper it to you when I think the time is right. Let's do it a few more times. On four ..."

CHAPTER TEN

Rehearsal

When you come to the end of a Perfect Day
And you sit alone with your thought
While the chimes ring out with a carol gay—

NORMA: Billy, you're singing a little flat on "carol." Once more, that line:

While the chimes ring out with a carol gay
For the joy that the day has brought.

BILLY: Better?
NORMA: Almost. Let's do it again.

*

LUCINDA: Are you sure we don't need a script?
BILLY: No script. We'll do a better act without one. Let's just have some ideas ready.

*

Lu stretches one leg after the other on the barre, a delicate foot pointed away from her. Billy hikes one slap-shoed foot up onto the barre in imitation, then the other, and holds on with his feet, suspended in the air for an impossible moment before crashing to the floor.

LUCINDA: Billy! Are you all right?
BILLY: I'm fine. Just roll your eyes and keep going.

*

*Down by the old mill stream where I first met you,
With your eyes of blue, dressed in gingham, too ...*

LUCINDA: Norma, do we still have those gingham dresses from a few years ago?
NORMA: I've got them packed away somewhere. We can let mine out if it's too small for you.
BILLY: Gingham? What's gingham? Sounds contagious.

*

Lucinda curtsies. Billy tries; pulls his pants pockets inside out and bobs his head. How to curtsy without a tutu? He strolls around nonchalantly, peers inside the piano lid, spots Lucinda's shawl hanging on the coat tree. While no-one's looking he sneaks the shawl and ties it around his waist, over his baggy trousers. He hangs his cap on the coat tree, rolls up his sleeves, spits on his palms. Lucinda glances at him and purses her lips as Billy takes a corner of the shawl in each hand, pinky fingers extended, and executes a deep and graceful curtsy.

*

LUCINDA: Can't we at least have a story?

BILLY: Here's your story: A boy sees a beautiful ballerina. Falls in love with her on the spot. Tries to win her affection, but not without causing a little trouble. The end.

*

Down by the old maelstrom, There'll be a calm before the storm ...

LUCINDA: What storm? And it's "mill stream," not "maelstrom."

BILLY: It's called parody. It's what I do, Lucinda-Lu.

*

Lucinda keeps her eye on a spot on the wall while she turns on one pointed toe, and at the last instant she whips her head around.

LUCINDA: It's called spotting. If I look at the same spot on the wall, I can keep turning without getting dizzy.

BILLY: Keep turning, I want to try something.

Billy watches Lucinda with interest, nods his head and tries a slow turn. He speeds up (all the while *not* spotting), and before long he is whirling around the stage, careening off the piano, knocking over the coat tree, and tripping over the barre until finally he flies into a series of aerial cartwheels. He loses his cap mid-air and crash-lands on it, seated on the floor and looking bewildered.

[61]

LUCINDA: Oh, Billy, are you hurt?

Billy rolls his eyes and flops onto his back, laughing.

*

Do you think what the end of a Perfect Day
Can mean to a tired heart ...

For a moment Billy stops what he's doing and listens. Her high notes never fail to pull every one of the hairs on the back of his neck to attention; it's as though he has never before understood the meaning of "a tired heart."

When the sun goes down with a flaming ray
and the dear friends have to part?

His throat tightens; he is in danger of making a fool of himself. Billy grabs the shawl from around his waist and dabs his eyes, covers his downturned mouth, and leans against the piano with his hand at his heart. He sniffles loudly, and as Lucinda holds the last note, he joins her in an unabashed howl. Norma is laughing so hard she can't finish playing the piece. Lucinda gives her a stern look.

*

LUCINDA: Will it be funny?
BILLY: Only if we keep it a half-step over from heartache.

CHAPTER ELEVEN

One-sheet

PASCOE & HART

TWO-ACT—SONG & DANCE, LIGHT COMEDY,
BALLET & ACROBATICS. PARODY.
*A Comedy Act, introducing singing, dancing,
light comedy, & parody. Good, clean comedy
guaranteed to meet all expectations, when a place
on the Bill is given. Mr. Pascoe & Miss Hart,
two young Stars of the Vaudeville Stage, will
bring the Boffo to delight the audience
with Mirth-provoking Situations.
Can close in One, if necessary.
Time: 15 min.*

"You're booked at Shea's Victoria in Toronto starting Monday. Influenza's left them with some holes in the bill, acts dropping like flies." Myra holds out the one-sheet for Billy to look at. "I've written to all the managers in the circuit. The three Bennetts Theatres are interested—that's Hamilton, Ottawa, and Montreal. Mr. Shea knows you can close in One, but until you two prove yourselves, the best you can hope for is fourth, or maybe sixth spot on the bill, try and settle the audience down after intermission."

"Thank you, Mrs. Pascoe," Lucinda says as she peers over Billy's shoulder to read the one-sheet.

"I can't imagine there's too many ballet comedy acts out there just now," Myra says. "But the best news of all, the entire route is two-a-day." She looks around the table at the three of them with satisfaction. "You won't wear yourselves out on three shows, six days a week."

"The Big Time, how wonderful!" Norma claps her hands.

"We'll be closing the first half in no time," Billy says.

"No-one's going to want to leave the theatre even to step outside for air once they've seen you two," Norma says, squeezing Lucinda's hand.

"Well, the quicker you break in the act, the sooner the other theatre managers'll hire you. Way I see it, you've got a week. They're all watching, you know." Myra lights a match and dips it into the bowl of her pipe. Billy looks at Lucinda while his mother's words settle, then he reaches in his pocket for his date book.

"I'll take care of the travel arrangements."

"Wait, where will we stay?" Lucinda looks at Billy, then at Norma, her eyes widening.

"Don't you worry about that," Myra says, "I'm going along with you as chaperone."

Billy opens his mouth to protest.

"Never you mind, you're not travelling alone with an underaged girl, Billy Pascoe. Lucinda and I'll take a room together and you can fend for yourself, maybe double up with one of the other acts on the bill. Where's your pal Lex Neal at these days, anyways?"

*

[64]

Lucinda takes Norma's arm as they walk through the woods to their cabin. The scent of woodsmoke follows them and their footsteps crunch as they step on curled leaves. She looks over at her sister, whose smile is a little bit tight around the edges.

"Norma, you can't stay here, it's too cold and you'll be all alone."

"Don't you worry about me, Lu, I'll be all right. Mr. and Mrs. Pike have invited me to join them in Toronto. Maybe I'll be able to see your show," she adds brightly.

"I'm going to miss you, Norma."

For a moment Norma doesn't reply. When she does, her voice catches in her throat.

"You and Billy are going to be an enormous success, I just know it," she finally says.

"Perhaps," Lucinda says, "But that doesn't mean I won't miss you terribly. You've been with me always."

"And we'll be together again soon. Remember that. Besides, you'll have Mrs. Pascoe there with you, thank goodness."

"It won't be the same."

"No, it won't," Norma says in a quiet voice. "But it's not supposed to be, is it? I mean, we're older now. We can't stay a young sister act forever."

Tree branches overhead rub together as the wind picks up.

"I wish we could." Lucinda holds Norma's hand as they hasten against the icy breeze. Soon they are trotting, then running the last bit of pathway to their cabin.

"Everything's different for Billy, too, now that he's

broken up the family act," Norma says. She reaches for the door and they rush inside.

While Norma heats the kettle over the wood stove, Lucinda recalls the sound of Billy's weeping, the sadness pouring off of him and into her arms as he grieved for his father, for the end of his family's act, and she knows now with certainty that nothing will ever be the same. Not for any of them.

CHAPTER TWELVE

Stage Fright

The walk across Richmond Street from the hotel has done nothing to calm Lucinda's nerves. At breakfast, while Billy gulped coffee and devoured a stack of pancakes, the most she had been able to manage to get around the fluttering bird in her chest was a small glass of milk. Already Myra has disappeared with her deck of cards and her pipe, gone off to find a pinochle game with the wife of one of the pit musicians.

"Come on, Lucinda, hurry up!" Billy urges her as he points across the street, where SHEA'S VICTORIA practically shouts from the marquee. Billy's rucksack is hanging from one shoulder and he has the dismantled prop-barre tucked under the other arm. He taps his foot waiting for a trolley to pass, and then there's a horse-drawn milk wagon and a few automobiles chugging along, by which point Billy is practically jumping up and down with the wait. If she had her way Lucinda would just stand there and allow them all to pass, one after another, all day long. But Billy has taken her by the elbow with his free hand and is weaving her in and out between carts, trolleys, and automobiles.

"Let's see who's on the bill," he says, his eyes lit with expectation as they approach the massive brick building. Billy hustles her around the corner and stops before the ornate frame hanging by the stage door.

[67]

— REFINED VAUDEVILLE —
ALWAYS A SHOW OF QUALITY
Ella Lola's Exotic & Titillating Turkish Dance
Fred Duprez, Monologist & Singing Comedian
Drama:
"Wives of the Rich,"
Mr. Clyde Gillingwater & Miss Edith Lyle
Pascoe & Hart, Ballet Comedy
Thurston the Great Magician
—INTERMISSION—

"They've put us right after the drama," Billy says with a gleam in his eye. "I could have fun with this."

Lucinda closes her eyes against a wave of nausea.

"You okay, Lu? You look kind of pale."

"I ... I'll be all right," she says. "I'm just a bit jittery."

"You'll be fine," he says as he opens the stage door. "Just you wait 'til you hear the applause tonight."

Lucinda gulps back another wave of nausea as she steps inside the theatre.

*

The stale air backstage holds the familiar scent of old sweat and talcum powder, their dressing room dimly lit by a single caged and flickering light bulb. It's just as well; Lucinda would prefer not to see too much in the way of the peeling paint and water stains on the ceiling, which does little to improve her sense of dread. She jumps as Billy slams the door open against the wall, pushing through with his arm-load of props.

[68]

"Lu, do you have Norma's lead-sheet handy? Mr. Peterson would like to see it."

"Of course," she says and she reaches for her bag, hoping her heart will slow its pounding. "Mr. Peterson is a fine pianist, I'm relieved to know he's here. He taught Norma when she was younger, you know."

"You ever learn piano?" Billy asks as he gives the prop-barre a final tightening.

"Yes, but Norma was so much quicker to learn, I sort of gave up. You?"

"I picked up a few tricks from Herb Williams between shows. Prefer to play the uke, though. Here, give me your foot."

Lucinda steps over to the barre and places her foot at one end while Billy leans on the other. The dowelling jiggles in its moorings.

"Where'd you learn to sing and dance?" Billy adjusts the clamp at his end and they try again. This time it holds.

"Mostly from my mother," Lucinda says. "But Norma was always after the ballerinas to show us proper technique. Some of them were very kind and patient with us. Sometimes, though, we just hid in the wings and imitated what they were doing during their warm-ups."

"That's how I learned, mostly, from watching. Houdini taught me a few card tricks, though."

"Harry Houdini? The Hand-cuff King?" Lucinda puts down the lead-sheet and stares at Billy.

"He's my godfather, you know," Billy says as he hefts the prop-barre onto one shoulder and opens the door. "You'd better take that upstairs to Mr. Peterson."

"But ... Harry Houdini?"

[69]

"I'll tell you after the show," Billy says, and he lifts his cap and dashes from the room.

With all the talking, Lucinda hasn't even thought about the show. With a lurch the bird begins to flap in her chest. Before it can take flight, she looks in the mirror, pinches her cheeks for colour, then grabs the lead-sheet and hurries out to the hallway and up the stairs. The bird can wait 'til after the rehearsal.

*

In silence, Billy powders his face with Hess. Lucinda finished making her face up ages ago; she glances at herself in the mirror and pretends not to watch as he outlines his eyes with Dark Brown No. 7, then brushes it along his eyebrows. When he reaches for the carmine to rub on his mouth, she looks away and hums a scale, up and then down. If only her voice won't wobble tonight.

"How d'you reach those high notes?" Billy asks, pressing his lips together, his stage face set. She is amazed at the difference; his regularly dark complexion is now a powdered opposite of itself with exaggerated features, his eyes fairly popping below expressive eyebrows while his mouth is muted, smaller.

"I don't know, they've always been there. It's Norma who's got the most beautiful alto voice, though. I'll never be able to sing the way she does."

Billy pauses with the carmine stick in hand, looks at her for a moment and then quickly sweeps his brushes and sticks into the makeup case.

"No-one can sing like you do, Lu," he says, and for a

moment Lucinda worries she'll blush through her face powder. He untucks the handkerchief from around his neck, shakes the stray powder from it, and clips his necktie in place. Billy is always moving, Lucinda thinks; he is never, ever still. Perhaps that's how he manages his nerves.

Before her own nerves threaten to get the better of her, she decides to run the act in her mind again. Maybe that'll calm her down.

"Tell me once more, Billy," she says. "Run it for me."

Billy looks at her reflection in the mirror.

"We start with you and Mr. Peterson on-stage," he says. "You begin your dance warm-up with him playing, and I'll follow with my broom, tidying up. Let me have a moment or two sweeping while I get a feel for the audience, then we'll get started."

"You won't change anything, will you?" Lucinda worries at a hangnail on her thumb.

"We'll do our business the same as we did in the clubhouse dining hall. But you know I'll be getting into trouble on my own. Just ignore me and keep doin' what you're doin', and I'll whisper your cues."

"Back-kick?"

"Yep," says Billy. "back-kick, pliés, and all the rest of them. It'll all be there, Lu. Trust me."

Billy turns in his chair to face her directly just as she rips the hangnail free of her thumb.

"Trust me, Lu."

His mouth turns upward slightly, but not too much, else he cracks the powder on his face. The pounding of pulse in her ears subsides. Of course she trusts him.

[71]

There is a discreet tap at the door, followed by the call boy's voice: "Five minutes, Pascoe and Hart."

"Pascoe and Hart, that's us," Billy whispers, his eyes dancing. "Thank you," he calls out, and it's just as well, as Lucinda is too busy slowing her breath to respond. When finally it slows, she looks up at Billy, who is now standing, pulling his suspenders into place.

"We still don't have a finish, Billy."

Billy shakes his head.

"You just break the audience's hearts with your version of *A Perfect Day*," he says. "I'll give you your finish."

He takes one last look at the dressing table, grabs a tin of boot-black and puts it in his pocket. He tugs his cap in place, winks at her, and holds the door open for her with a sweeping bow. Lucinda stands up, prays her legs will carry her up the stairs, gathers her tutu so it won't catch in the door, and dashes into the hallway.

CHAPTER THIRTEEN

New Act

She has done her pliés, hit him in the nose and kicked him in the pants, ignored his attention, spurned him; they have sung together, he has climbed on top of the piano and jumped off in a forward flip mid-song. At least she thinks so. There has been a blur of laughter, from titters to belly laughs, but it can only have been for Billy, Boffo Billy, the Funniest Boy in Vaudeville.

All of this races through her mind as Lucinda holds her last note floating high and clear over the top of the stage, her eyes closed against the glare of the footlights and the audience she knows is watching her. There is not a sound, not a rustle in the theatre; she doesn't know where Billy is. He could be anywhere behind her, or who knows, maybe he's left the stage.

She has held the note for as long as she can, and now she lets it go and it drifts up into the rafters. Lucinda lowers her head and opens her eyes. He is beside her, on the floor on bended knee, his hands at his sides and a look of naked sadness in his eyes that she has seen only once, weeks and a lifetime ago in the boathouse. This is the heartache; Billy is showing her the half-step over from comedy.

She faces her audience, sighs, and looks down at him sorrowfully. Leans over and kisses Billy on the cheek. A titter emerges from the audience as he rises slowly from kneeling, his mouth opened in astonishment and his hand at his cheek where she kissed him. With a sudden blink at his good fortune, he grabs her by the wrist and leads her into the wings, stage right, her free hand held over her mouth as she casts a doubtful look at the audience. They titter knowingly. If only they knew how terrified she really was.

*

"Mess up your lip-rouge, quick," Billy says as he pulls the tin of boot-black from his pocket and unscrews the lid. "Make like I've kissed you, then slap me."

"What do you mean, slap you?" Lucinda freezes.

"Never mind, I'll do the slap. Mess up your mouth, quick, then count to five before you go back out. Hurry!"

"What ... I'm going back out?"

"Just walk across the stage, measured-like. I'll follow you. Trust me, they'll love it."

In the semi-darkness of the wings she runs a shaking finger over her mouth, smudging her lip rouge while he rubs boot-black around his left eye. She nods her readiness and he claps his hands once in a pretend-slap—his hands are larger and louder than hers—and then he falls over a nearby chair and lands hard, pounding his fists and slap-shoes on the floor for extra noise. She is puzzled—did he really need to fall?

"Believable," he says as he stands. "Ready? Count to five first. Then knock 'em dead."

She nods and breathes around the bird in her chest. Billy knows timing better than anyone; she trusts him. Counts to five, slowly.

She marches onstage, glares back at the wings, sniffs at the audience. The titter has grown to a yowl that follows her as she stalks off stage left. They laughed! The bird slows its flapping wings.

He follows her, stumbling, clutching the left side of his face. A broken hat brim dangles around his neck, and his hair is mussed. He stares helplessly after her and lowers his hand; as he turns and looks balefully toward the foot-lights, the audience catches sight of his black eye and gives him a belly laugh.

Applause; curtain.

She has fixed her lip rouge. They hold hands—friends again—and together they bow. One curtain call, not bad for their first show together.

*

Wednesday Matinee: Fifth Show ... He grabs her by the wrist and leads her into the wings, stage right, her free hand held over her mouth in mock-horror. The audience chortles. Offstage she smudges her lip rouge, and he pokes at the boot-black. He looks at her with dark, unreadable eyes. "You do it," he says, holding out the tin, "Last night I made a mess of it." She hesitates. It's true, he had boot-black halfway up his forehead. "C'mon, hurry. Please?" She dips into the tin, pats and then swirls the black around his eye. Tries to ignore the feel of his cheekbone beneath her hand. Where to wipe her fingers? She bites her lip and slaps lightly at his cheek, leaving the mark of her hand, a black imprint against white powder. His eyes widen and he grins;

[75]

the bird leaps in her chest as it does the moment before she first walks onstage.

The sound of his hand-clap startles her—it shouldn't, but it does—and his tumble onto the floor, louder than usual, gets her counting her beats faster than she ought. She strides onstage, prays she looks indignant, hopes the flush creeping up her throat toward her face won't show beneath her makeup.

*

Friday Evening: Tenth Show ... He grabs her by the wrist and leads her into the wings, stage right, her free hand held over her mouth as she tries not to giggle. The Friday night crowd is hooting and hollering, chasing them with guffaws and whistles from the gallery. Offstage she starts to rub her finger over her lips. "Wait," he says, and before she can stop him he has reached over to help, his thumb burning a trail on the skin around her mouth. "Better," he says, and she can't help but notice his Adam's apple jumping behind his collar, his unblinking eyes dark as velvet. Once again she helps blacken his eye while tiny drops of sweat glitter through his powder in the semi-darkness. Without breaking his gaze on her, he claps his hands and falls over the chair to the floor. "Believable," she thinks, as she counts to five over the thudding of her heart.

*

Saturday Night: Twelfth Show ... He grabs her by the wrist and leads her into the wings, stage right, her free hand held over her mouth, her heart already racing. The air is different tonight, crackling and charged with light. She flirts with the audience, tosses them a wink as she steps into the wings. Beyond the footlights they clap and guffaw; someone fires off a wolf whistle.

In the shadows he pulls her hand away from her mouth and holds it down by her side. He stands close and settles his free hand against her throat—such a warm hand, she thinks—and he leans in, pressing his lips to hers. For a long moment everything is quiet and still; even the breath in her has stilled while his mouth roams and nudges and her legs turn to water. Then he steps back and holds her in his dark eyes, his face smeared with her lip rouge. "Believable," he says in a low voice, and as he brings his hands together and claps her pretend-slap like gunshot, she sees his un-blackened eye. The boot-black, where is the boot-black? But it's too late; he has fallen and she must count to five. She points at her eye, then at him, and he is sprawled on the floor resting on one elbow, his face hidden in the shadows. She counts and hopes for the best.

Tonight feels different: The two of them, the audience, the crackling air. It's Saturday night and the crowd is waiting to see what she will do next. Hands on hips, she swings beneath her corset as she walks back onstage, giving him time. She pauses mid-stage and looks over her shoulder. He is watching her with a smudged half-smile, the broken hat dangling around his neck and his eye rimmed with black. She lifts her chin, rolls her eyes at the audience, and languidly makes her way to stage left and into the wings to the swell of laughter. Three beats and he's stumbling after her, tripping once, twice, picking up speed and then diving over the piano stool and landing in a somersault on the floor by her feet. With his fingers he counts off three more beats, and then he sends the broken hat brim spinning high above the empty stage. The audience roars a boffo laugh. Applause and the shriek of whistles fill the air.

Curtain.

He takes her by the hand and she follows him, lips in disarray. She curtsies deeply. He kisses her hand and bows at her and she curtsies again. Four curtain calls.

CHAPTER FOURTEEN

Bookings

"You've surely got yourselves some more bookings," Myra says without raising her eyes. She lays her cards one by one on the makeup counter while Billy kicks a chair out of the way and dives into a handstand. He is practically electric from tonight's show, and he needs to pump some of the charge out of himself. He walks on his hands over to the wall where he rests his feet and pushes up and down until his shoulders ache.

"Says who?" he asks as he counts off five more push-ups.

"I just know it," Myra says. "There's agents from Black's and Pantages out there tonight, I saw them comin' in the stage door after the second act. Terrible, by the way; who does that Mr. Duprez think he is, droning on and on without an ounce of wit? And where's Lucinda?"

"She stopped at the Ladies' room." Billy lowers his legs slowly in a vee, and hops to his feet. "She really trouped tonight, Ma, even the ushers came out to watch her. You could have heard a pin drop at the end of *A Perfect Day*. Then she went big and got a good belly laugh at her exit."

"Yeah, well I'd say she got something," Myra says. Billy looks over at his mother's reflection, her eyes on him like spotlights. Surely she didn't see him kissing Lu offstage.

There is a knock at the partly-opened door, and Lucinda steps inside the dressing room, the lower half of her face wiped clean. She pulls the chair over to the mirror and unscrews the cold cream jar.

"Hello, Mrs. Pascoe," she says quietly as she starts rubbing cream on her forehead.

"Billy says you did a fine job, Lucinda. You got some good laughs tonight." Myra slips her deck of cards into her purse and points at her coat, which Billy removes from the hook and holds while she slides her arms in the sleeves. "I was telling him there were some agents in the audience; you two are bound to get booked after tonight. Just be careful that boy of mine don't ask too much of you," she says, giving him a sideways glance. "I have an appointment with the O'Connor Sisters; we've got a poker game started in their dressing room. I'll see you back at the hotel."

Billy holds the door for his mother, then turns to face Lucinda. She points at him and shakes her head and he looks at his reflection. Her lip rouge is smeared all over his mouth.

*

A dusting of snow covers the sidewalk and quickly powders their coats. Lucinda adjusts her hat and Billy tucks the prop-barre and his rucksack under one arm, then offers her his other arm.

"Might be icy underfoot," he says as she rests her hand in the crook of his elbow. "Good show tonight," he says. "And Ma was right, we got some bookings. You ought to cable Norma and tell her we'll be on the road for a few weeks. I'll arrange tickets and hotels first thing tomorrow—there's a mid-morning train we can take to Hamilton. You ever play

[80]

at Bennett's? Nice theatre, but the backstage is tiny. It can be hectic between acts."

"Billy, this is the most I've heard you speak at one time," Lucinda says smiling up at him.

"Yeah, well, sometimes I get a little talky after a show. Only thing I've got to watch for is your back-kick; I nearly missed it in the pants tonight."

"That was my fault, I should have kicked harder."

"You know you can really give it to me, don't you, Lu?"

"I know," she says. "I'm just not accustomed to kicking someone in the backside."

"Well, get used to it," Billy says, "The audience loves it. And they love your singing, too. Pin-drop silence like that happens once in a blue moon."

They stop at the corner and wait for some automobiles to pass. Lucinda's face caught in the street light is the prettiest thing Billy has ever seen, he thinks, as snowflakes settle on her eyelashes.

"I liked kissing you," he says suddenly, and she blinks and looks at the ground. "I mean ... I hope you didn't mind it, but ... I liked it."

"Billy," she says, finally looking up at him, "I liked it too, but I don't think it's a good idea, making it part of the act."

"No-one said it has to be part of the act," he says, and immediately wonders why he is talking so much.

"I meant to say, Billy ..."

An auto has stopped and is waiting to let them cross. Billy hoists the barre and leads Lucinda across the street perhaps a little too hastily; she is nearly running when they reach the curb. He has said the wrong thing, and far too much of it. His mind races to make up for his stupid chatter.

"I'll bring a stick of carmine with me and leave it offstage with the boot-black," he says in a rush. "We can do it that way instead."

"Billy, I ..."

"It'll only take a few seconds longer, but I'll shorten the fall over the chair, and ..."

"Billy, let me ..."

"... then you can count your five beats and ..."

"Billy!"

Lucinda stops suddenly and nearly pulls him off-balance with the force of it. He only just keeps the pieces of prop-barre from tumbling to the ground. When finally he can bring himself to look at her he is relieved in a way that her face is in shadow. Tiny snowflakes drift slowly downward in the lamplight behind her.

"I just want to say thank you. For kissing me, I mean. It helped, it really did; I couldn't have made that exit without it."

Billy opens his mouth to speak but no words come out.

"You've been helping me all week, and before, too, when we were rehearsing. I just want to tell you how grateful I am. And Norma is, too."

Lucinda slips her hand in the crook of his elbow and starts walking again.

"Now, you promised me you'd tell me about Harry Houdini. Did you really mean it when you said he's your godfather?"

Billy lets out the breath he'd been holding, relieved at the sudden change in subject.

"It's true," he says. "Harry and my folks toured together

in a travelling medicine show. Pop did his eccentric dances and backflips while Ma played her saxophone solos, and Houdini wowed the crowd with his card tricks. He was the so-called doctor who hawked Kickapoo Elixir for a dollar a bottle, six fer' five—'Good for everything from the barber's itch to galloping consumption,' he'd tell 'em. I was born one night on the tour, practically backstage; been in the theatre ever since."

"And where were you born?"

"Some little town in Kansas that's not there anymore. A few months after we left, it was blown away by a cyclone."

"Oh, Billy, you're making that up." Lucinda squeezes his arm.

"No word of a lie, I am not making it up," Billy says. "A cyclone lifted it right off the map. Ever been to Kansas during cyclone season?"

"You make me laugh, Boffo Billy."

She is still laughing and Billy is breathing more easily as they walk up the steps to the hotel.

"Evening, Miss Hart, Mr. Pascoe," says the doorman. "Was it a good crowd tonight?"

"Full house, thanks," Billy says as he follows Lucinda through the door. Once inside he takes off his cap and shakes the snow off it, and stamps some warmth into his feet.

"I'll walk you to your room," he says.

"That's all right, I can manage. You've got all that to carry."

"Well, I'll see you at breakfast, then. I'll arrange for the train tickets, try for mid-morning."

"And I'll notify Norma," Lucinda says. Then she smiles at him. "It's been an exciting week. I'm looking forward to the next one."

"You're a real corker, Lu," he says, "The audience loves you."

"I'm quite sure you're the corker, Billy. I just follow along."

Billy shrugs and shifts his rucksack to the other shoulder.

"Good night, Billy."

Swiftly as a bird, she stands on tiptoe and kisses him on the cheek. Then she is gone, hurrying down the hallway.

CHAPTER FIFTEEN

Toronto Daily Star

DECEMBER 4TH, 1916—The Christmas season approaches and folks have on a holiday mood. If there's one thing in vaudeville calculated to afford a good natured, wholesome scream of delight, it's the antics of Pascoe & Hart. Regular vaudeville patrons have seen Boffo Billy Pascoe grow up upon the stage. When he was a youngster his father threw him around unmercifully and now he is a young man. Starring alongside him is the lovely Lucinda Hart, ballerina and soprano extraordinaire. It's a slapstick parody act paired with the best of song and dance, and it delighted the Shea's Victoria Toronto audience.

CHAPTER SIXTEEN

Fireman's Lift

"Break a leg, you two," Myra urges them through a puff of pipe smoke. Billy holds the dressing room door open for Lucinda, who darts out the door and then back in again, practically knocking Billy over as the stage hands rush past carrying a set of canvas flats.

"I told you it's hectic back here," Billy says. "You ready?"

Lucinda nods and takes a shaky breath.

"Just a little nervous," she says. "Opening night again."

"Don't worry, it's just like any other Monday." Billy gives her a gentle nudge and she steps into the wings.

"And now, ladies and gem'men, two young vaudeville stars with a fresh new act, Pascoe and Hart!"

The pianist commences playing. Lucinda straightens her back, smoothes her tutu, takes a deep breath, and walks onstage to the barre. A ripple of applause reaches her from the darkness beyond the footlights; she rests her hand on the barre and moves her arm to the music, stretching it in an arc above her head, then moving her left foot to the front, to the side, to the back. Again.

There is more applause and an appreciative murmur, and she knows Billy has sauntered onstage with his broom, seemingly unaware of her, of the audience. Behind her he is sweeping here and there, she knows, inspecting the piano, lifting the shawl hanging on the coat tree and letting it down again, sweeping some more. Titters and chuckles float over the footlights, and suddenly there is a guffaw. He has seen her, perhaps has clutched his hand to his chest and rolled his eyes in appreciation. The audience is laughing. They now know the story: The boy is in love with the ballerina, and he must somehow win her affection. Lucinda ignores Billy and carries on with her stretches.

He builds the gags one after the other, brings the audience up the ladder of laughs to the top rung, and now it is her turn. She holds her final note and nothing feels safer than this, singing her soul to the audience, until she casts her eyes down to Billy, who is sprawled on the floor next to her where he has landed in a spectacular pratfall, with his hand at his heart and a look of utter love-struck helplessness. She helps him to his feet and regards him as though for the first time, then kisses him on the cheek. He turns and faces the audience, his mouth opened in astonishment and his hand at his cheek. With a sudden blink at his good fortune, he grabs her by the wrist and leads her into the wings, stage right, her free hand held over her mouth as she casts a doubtful look at the audience. They titter knowingly.

*

In the semi-darkness of the wings she runs a finger over her mouth, smudging her lip-rouge while he rubs boot-black around his left eye. He reaches for the stick of carmine, but knocks it from the chair to the floor where it lands with a crack like gunshot. The sound of it rolling away into the shadows seems to echo through the theatre. Billy looks at her, wild-eyed, and makes as though to dive to the floor, but she grabs his shoulder first and kisses him hard on the lips. For a moment he stares at her, not moving.

"Clap, Billy," she whispers, and he does, and as he falls over the chair she turns to count five. In the same instant her foot catches something on the floor and suddenly it is rolling, taking her with it. She puts out her arm to break her fall, and the carmine stick rolls out onstage just as the pain shoots up from her wrist and past her elbow to her shoulder and back down again.

"Lucinda, you all right?"

She cannot speak for fear of screaming in pain, but she nods her head and lets him help her to her feet.

"Your knee's bleeding. I'll carry you out."

Billy grabs hold of her arm—not the one that's on fire, thank the lord—and drapes her over his shoulders. She hopes the audience can't see the blood as he carries her, fireman's lift, across the stage. She manages a wave and a wink at the audience, and they clap and cheer their approval. Somehow, Billy gets her to the stageleft wings and eases her onto a chair.

"Get some ice, quick," she hears him say to the stage manager. She is in a daze of pain as the sting in her knee kicks in on top of the throbbing in her arm.

"It's my wrist, Billy, I've hurt my wrist."

"Mr. Pascoe, they want a bow," says the stage manager, and he is right, the audience has erupted in sustained applause. Billy looks at her with his eyebrows raised.

"I can do it," she says, and he helps her to her feet and they take three steps onstage. Her tutu covers her bloodied knee and she curtsies, leaning heavily against Billy's hand. He bows to her and to the audience, and then with his hand at her waist he leads her offstage where the stage manager is waiting with the ice.

*

Billy half-carries her down the stairs to the dressing room, and she limps over to the chair by the mirror. Myra looks up from her card game and lifts her eyebrows.

"I didn't mean for you to actually break your leg," she says.

"Ma!" Billy glares at her.

Lucinda can't help herself; she is on the brink of tears, but Myra's words bring the absurdity of the situation burbling up from deep inside. She rests her head on her one good arm and sobs enormous gusts of laughter.

"Aw, Lu, please don't cry. Here, let me put the ice pack on your wrist, and I'll wrap your knee up. Everything's going to be fine."

Billy is bustling around her, trying to fix it all. She looks up at him with a wet smile, and the sight of his face, earnest and slightly ill at ease, brings about the tears she's been holding back and she is in a sudden wash of weepy giggles. Billy's eyes widen with confusion and he looks over at his mother for help.

"Find some water and a towel, Billy, and I'll take care of that knee. Go on, Lucinda'll be safe with me," Myra says, handing Billy the wash bowl, and Billy hurries out the door.

"Seems to me you need a female shoulder to cry on, dear. You just go right on ahead." Myra pulls her chair next to Lucinda's and holds out her arms; Lucinda nestles her head on Myra's thin shoulder and after a few moments her sobbing abates to sniffles.

"You're right, Mrs. Pascoe," she says. "I was just thinking how I wish Norma were here."

There is a knock, and Billy peers around the door.

"Come in, Billy, it's safe now," Lucinda says.

"Let's get those stockings off her and I'll clean that knee up. You look the other way, now, but give her your arm for balance. That's it. Now, hand me the iodine. The last thing you need is an infection, Lucinda. Take hold of Billy, this'll sting a little."

Lucinda sucks in her breath as the iodine burns into her leg, and as she grabs Billy's hand he falls to his knees with his eyes crossed in mock-agony. In spite of herself, Lucinda smiles at the sight of him writhing on the floor, gasping and clutching his hand.

"I'll never use it again," he moans.

"Done," Myra says, and she wraps a bandage around Lucinda's knee. "It's that wrist that's a worry. We'll bind it for tonight and see how it looks in the morning. Billy, you take care of that and I'll go check in with the stage manager. You'll have to make some changes to the act. You've got some binding tape in your bag, haven't you?"

*

"It's not too swollen," he says as he eases the tape around her wrist.

"Your mother's right, we're going to have to make some changes," Lucinda says. "I'm so sorry, Billy."

"I'm the one who's sorry," he says. "It was me knocking the carmine off the chair that did it."

"And I'm the fool who stepped on it. It was just a silly accident," Lucinda says. "I'll need to reverse my position on the barre so I'm not holding it with my right hand."

"That's easy." Billy turns her hand over and wraps the tape around her palm. "If need be we'll just switch the stage set-up, put the piano stage right and leave the coat tree in the middle."

"Will there be time to sort that out before the matinee?"

"I'll come in first thing tomorrow morning and talk to the stage manager. He knows we'll be making a few changes. Not too tight?" he holds up Lucinda's hand for her inspection.

"It's fine, thanks. Feels much better," Lucinda says, and it does feel better now that it's bound.

"Let's see you walk," Billy says as he helps her to her feet. She leans against him and limps across the dressing room to the door. "Now, by yourself," he says, and as she hobbles back to the chair, Billy frowns.

"It'll probably loosen up by tomorrow, but we may need another song, just in case," he says.

"That's all right, Norma just sent me some new song sheets," Lucinda says. "I can have one or two of them learned by tomorrow. I'll come in early and rehearse them with the pianist."

"You sure that's enough time?" Billy says.

"I'm sure," Lucinda says, and she pushes aside the nagging doubt. "I've heard them both before; it's just a matter of memorizing the words. Now, you go on back to the hotel while I clean myself up and hang up my costume."

"I'll get changed in the Men's room," Billy says as he picks up his street clothes. "Don't go anywhere, you'll need some help walking back."

"Oh, Billy," Lucinda calls out. "Let's make one more change." Billy pauses in the doorway. "No more carmine?"

A small smile takes shape on Billy's face. "No more carmine," he says.

CHAPTER SEVENTEEN

Sixters

336 Brunswick, Toronto
December 6, 1916

My Darling Lu,

*Mrs. Pascoe has kindly forwarded me your itinerary,
so that I may follow your travels. I've seen the marvelous
write-up in the Toronto Daily Star and couldn't be prouder
of my little sister. If only I could see for myself the wonderful job you are doing with Billy! I'm sure you hold the audience in the palm of your hand every time you open your
mouth to sing.*

*I am now settled at Lizzie and David Pikes' house in
Toronto, alas, a few days too late to have seen you play the
Victoria. How well I remember that theatre, where you and
I have performed on occasion. I would be the first to hop
on a train to Hamilton to see you and Billy trouping at
Bennett's, but the doctor has advised against travel for the
remainder of my confinement. I've had one or two worri-
some moments—nothing for you to trouble yourself over—
so I am taking his good advice for the next couple of months
and staying in one place.*

*It is very comfortable here, and Lizzie Pike is being very
kind. She and David have the most adorable little girls,
Natalie and Constance, who take great pleasure in singing*

their little songs to me. They remind me of us when we were small and Mother would play the piano while we pranced and sang "Ta-ra-ra Boom-de-ay." Do you remember? Well, it's much the same here. I take great pleasure in playing the piano for the girls, and it is a good distraction for them, as David is now at the front lines going on six months and they miss him terribly. I do what I can to help.

I thought you might be interested in looking at these song sheets, in case you want to make some changes to your act. I know how Billy likes to keep things moving. "I Love You Truly" may be a good choice for you to end the act, once your ballerina has discovered her true feelings for the boy. In any case, Miss Jacobs-Bond's "Seven Songs as Unpretentious as the Wild Rose" collection is sure to have a few treasures.

By the way, does Billy still sing "carol" flat? (I'm joking, of course. He has a fine baritone and it plays beautifully with your soprano.)

I'll finish this letter now and send it to you with kisses and great pride in my little sister. I know well that this has not been easy for you, and I am grateful to you and to Billy for all your hard, hard work.

I do miss you, dear, and I look forward to seeing you soon. All my love,
Norma

PS—And speaking of songs, see if Billy knows one called "Where Did You Get That Hat?" It may give him some ideas. I'll see if I can find it at the song shop on Church Street.

*

Lucinda folds the letter, which she has now read four times, and places it on the dresser. How she misses Norma, wishes she were here with her especially tonight. She sighs and pulls the song sheets from the envelope and lays open "I Love You Truly."

I love you truly, truly dear,
Life with its sorrow, life with its tears
Fades into dreams when I feel you are near
For I love you truly, truly dear.

Ah! Love, 'tis something to feel your kind hand
Ah! Yes, 'tis something by your side to stand;
Gone is the sorrow, gone doubt and fear,
For you love me truly, truly dear.

"Gone is the sorrow, gone doubt and fear," brings her the prickle of tears. Lucinda allows herself a moment, then she wipes her eyes and studies the words. Surely she'll learn them by morning.

CHAPTER EIGHTEEN

Snapshots

1. PUBLICITY: A young couple pose in a photographer's studio with drapery hung behind them, an oriental carpet on the floor. She is dressed in a ballerina's costume, balancing on one leg with a hand on the back of a chair, holding her arm overhead in a graceful arc with the other leg extended behind. She is unaware of the young man behind her, dressed in baggy trousers, suspenders, slap-shoes and cap, holding a broomstick with one hand and with his other hand to his head as though scratching it in puzzlement. He is staring solemnly at her pointed toe, utterly absorbed.

2. MAKEUP: In profile. The young woman sits at the makeup table, dressed in a pale tutu with a shawl draped over her bare shoulders. From a single, caged light bulb above the mirror, a harsh shaft of light falls on her face as the young man leans toward her holding a makeup stick before her left eye. His profile shows a face intent and solemn. Out of sight of the viewer, the stick reads *Dark Brown No. 7*. Also out of sight of the viewer is the young woman's right wrist, bound and held at her side.

3. IN THE WINGS: They stand in shadow, their white-powdered faces softened by ambient light from the stage. There is an air of readiness about them; the young woman holds a stillness in her eyes, while standing behind her, the young man has the look of one who has just drawn a sharp breath, steeling himself.

4. BILLIARDS: The girl stands in a plié at one end of the barre, oblivious to the boy who has lined up his broomstick against an imaginary billiards ball he has balanced at the other end of the barre.

5. PAGE-TURNER: The girl stands poised beside the upright piano with her eyes closed and her mouth opened in song, hands crossed before her. The boy is sitting on top of the piano watching her with a look of adoration while he holds up the sheet music behind him, upside-down, for the pianist to read. The pianist glares from his seat on the piano stool.

6. FLIP-FLAP: The girl stands centre-stage with her arms outstretched, facing the audience, again with her eyes closed and her mouth opened in song. Behind her on stageleft, the boy hangs suspended upside-down in the air at an impossible height, his cap a blur flying off to one side.

7. PRATFALL: The boy lies sprawled on the floor with his legs in the air and his eyebrows raised in surprise,

while the girl stands nearby with her hands on her hips, her lips pursed and eyes rolled.

8. EPIPHANY: The girl stares at the boy as she pulls him up, rump-first, by the seat of his trousers. He has a look of bewilderment on his face. Unseen by the viewer: the boy is pushing himself up by every means to ease the strain on the girl's wrist.

9. BOWS: The boy holds the girl by the left hand as she sweeps the floor with her tutu in a curtsy. There is a faint sepia smudge at the corner of his lip.

10. FINI: In profile. The young woman is sitting once again at the makeup table, on which there is a dripping bag of ice. The young man sits facing her, this time with her right forearm in hand, wrapping her wrist in binding tape. They are both dressed in street-clothes, she in a simple, dark skirt and blouse, he in trousers and a pullover. She has her mouth opened in delight as though laughing, and his lips show a slight upward curve while his head is bent to his task.

CHAPTER NINETEEN

Lay-off

"I've got your route sorted out for the New Year," Myra says, "Five weeks through New Jersey and New York State, starting at Black's Theatre in Syracuse. There's a week's layoff I'll try to fill in Boston, then you're back up to Canada for a three-week run on the east coast. You'll have some long travel days, but it's two months' work you didn't have before."

"Oh, Mrs. Pascoe, this is wonderful news," Lucinda says, as she snaps her suitcase shut.

"How'd you get us into Black's?" Billy picks up the suitcase and swings it on top of the growing pile on the hotel cart.

"Wasn't easy," Myra says. "That Robert Black holds a grudge even though it was his brother Samuel your Pop chased out of the theatre."

Billy glances at Myra, then Lucinda. The mere mention of Samuel Black tightens the knot in his gut. He'll never forget the sense of helpless rage as he stood alone onstage while his father's bellows rang though the hall as he chased Black out the stage door and into the bustle of New York City.

"But Bob Black knows you two are a draw. He reads the trades," Myra says. "You be on your best behaviour, Billy, or he'll fire you so fast you won't know what hit you when he slams the stage door on you. He'll be reporting back to Samuel in New York the minute you take your bows." Myra eyes Lucinda. "And you be on your toes, missy. Bob Black has an eye for the young ladies and a slippery hand, at that."

Billy clenches his jaw and heaves the last suitcase onto the pile, which nearly topples with the extra force.

"Meanwhile, we've got a week in Toronto to rest up and get organized," Myra says. "It'll do your wrist some good, Lucinda."

"And I plan to learn some new songs." Lucinda lays her coat across the pile of suitcases and buttons up her boots. "Norma's bought some new song-sheets for me to look at. What'll you do with your time, Billy?"

"Probably watch some flickers." Billy is glad of the change of subject. "I'd like to see *Intolerance* one more time. You seen it?"

"No, but I hear it's marvelous."

"Why don't you let me take you to see it? Surely there's a movie house near where Norma's staying."

"I'd love to, Billy, thank you."

*

The morning sun hangs white in the dull winter sky, peering over the peaked roofs of Brunswick Avenue. There are wreaths hanging on doors and footprints in the snow along the sidewalks. Billy tips the taxi driver and lifts the two largest suitcases from the running board, following his mother up the steps to the porch where the doorway is crowded with Lucinda and Norma caught in a tearful embrace.

"Billy!" Norma cries as he lowers the suitcases and holds out his arms to her. The Norma who makes her way slowly over to him is a much older version than he remembers from four short weeks ago; her face is thin and pale, and her shoulders stooped. A loose-fitting housecoat hangs off her shoulders, and a wrap conceals the growing baby.

"Oh, Billy, it's so good to see you," Norma says as she reaches for him. Billy carefully places a hand on her shoulder and leans down to kiss her cheek. She looks so fragile, he is afraid she may break.

"How are you, Norma?" he asks, and she gives him a weary smile.

"Oh, I've been better," she says. "I'll tell you more, but first let's get you inside. Leave the cases there, I'll show you your rooms later. Lizzie's made lunch, and the girls are so excited—they can't wait to meet Boffo Billy."

Billy steps inside and fills his lungs with the scent of roasting chicken.

"I sure could do with a home-cooked meal," he says, suddenly ravenous for the intimacy of eating around a table with family and friends, a break from the monotony of diner meals on the road.

Lunch is a noisy, happy affair filled with much chatter from the two little girls, who can't stay away from Billy. He keeps busy showing them tricks, and soon the three of them are sitting in a row with spoons hanging off the ends of their noses.

"Norma, look at me!" Constance, the younger child cries, and Norma smiles from across the table. Deep shadows line her cheeks below her eyes, and she picks at the roast chicken and carrots on her plate.

"May we sing now, Norma?" asks Natalie, the older girl.

Lizzie Pike stands up and takes her daughters by the hand and leads them out of the dining room. "Why don't you girls go and rehearse your dance number, and we'll be along shortly. I'm sure Lucinda and Billy will be delighted to see your little show."

Lucinda casts a worried look at Norma, then at Lizzie.

"There, now, we can have a little quiet. Why don't I leave the three of you to visit? Mrs. Pascoe, would you like me to show you your room? I imagine you're tired from the train ride and all the noise around here."

"Thank you, Lizzie, and for the delicious lunch," says Myra. "I'm about ready for a little nap. But be sure to come find me when your mother-in-law gets back; we've got some cards to play."

Lizzie closes the door behind her and the dining room is suddenly quiet.

"I'll put the kettle on and we can visit," Norma says, and as she slowly stands, her wrap falls away from her shoulders. Billy tries not to look, but where he expects to glimpse the roundness of her belly, there is nothing. Norma's housecoat hangs straight down to the floor.

Billy tries to speak, only to find the words gone dry in his mouth. Instead, Lucinda's voice fills the silence. "Oh, Norma, what happened?" The blood has drained from Lucinda's cheeks and her eyes are enormous. "Darling, are you all right?"

Norma offers Lucinda a wan smile and sits back down in her chair.

"I'm fine, Lucinda, just a little tired," she says. "Two

weeks ago I lost the baby. I didn't want to worry you while you were touring."

"You should be in bed, Norma," Lucinda says as she grasps Norma's hand. "What does the doctor say?"

"He says I'm to rest when I'm tired, and drink plenty of fluids."

"And so you must," Lucinda says. She lays her hand on her sister's cheek and Norma leans into it with her eyes closed.

"I'll make the tea." Billy jumps up from his chair, grateful for the words that have finally come, relieved to be able to do something useful.

Just then a peal of laughter rings through the house, and the little girls rush into the dining room.

"Oh, Billy, Boffo Billy, we love you, true," they sing in two-part harmony.

"You go on with the girls, Billy, and I'll make the tea," Lucinda says, and before he can protest, Natalie grabs one hand and Constance the other, and they are dragging him up the stairs.

*

The next day Billy offers to take the girls with him to find a Christmas tree. Myra and Mrs. Pike are happy to reminisce over a game of cards, while Lucinda and Lizzie run some errands and Norma bakes cookies. Billy is glad of the cold air, of the company of children.

"Uncle Billy, will you carry me, please?" Constance peers up at him from beneath her woolen hat, all eyelashes and sparkling brown eyes. The instant he swings her up onto his shoulders, there is a tug at his hand and he looks down to see that Natalie has grabbed his thumb.

"I ought to hold your hand when we cross the street," she says solemnly. He wraps his hand around her tiny mitten, and starts to hum.

"You girls know a little song called *Jingle Bells*?" he asks.

Constance sings at the top of her lungs from her perch on his shoulders, and Natalie's sweet treble fills out over Billy's baritone as they make their way through the snow to the tree lot. He is filled with a rare lightness, happy to sing and clown with the little Pike sisters, free of the responsibility of the stage.

After he pays for the tree, he reaches down and plucks a penny from Natalie's ear, then Constance's.

"Magic!" she cries.

The proprietor smiles at the girls, then at Billy.

"Your daddy is a magician," he says, and hands them both a candy cane, which distracts the girls from correcting him. Billy is just as glad; for a moment he is happy to think of the girls as being his, of being their father. A pang of longing strikes him, surprising in its intensity, as he thinks how his life might be someday: children, a wife. A home of his own. He hoists Constance back up on his shoulders, lifts Natalie onto the middle of the tree, and grabbing hold of the trunk, he tramps through the snow, whistling.

*

Billy tosses a log in the fireplace and watches the sparks fly up the chimney. The sitting room is filled with the scent of pine, taking him for a moment to the Muskoka woods in summer.

"It's a lovely tree, Billy," Lizzie says to him while she hangs an ornament on a high branch. "Thank you for taking the girls along with you. They're glad of a man in the house, what with their father being overseas."

"I think the girls are madly in love with you," Norma says from her seat on the wing chair.

"Seems to me the feeling is mutual." Lucinda smiles and tucks a cover around Norma's shoulders.

"They're cute kids. Nice little singers, too," Billy says. "That Connie is a real corker, and Natalie sings like an angel."

Lizzie beams and looks over at Norma, who smiles and rests her head against the back of the chair.

"That's Norma's doing; she's spent a lot of time at the piano with them."

Lucinda unwraps a gold-painted glass star. "We should all sing carols tomorrow night before the girls go to bed," she says. "We used to do that every Christmas Eve, didn't we, Norma. Norma?"

Lizzie puts her finger to her lips and points to the sleeping figure, curled and tiny under the blanket.

"She's had a busy day," Lizzie says quietly.

"Lizzie, I'm so grateful to you for taking care of her," Lucinda says. "If only I'd known, I'd have been here in an instant."

"Which is why she didn't say anything until you arrived here for Christmas," Lizzie says. "Norma didn't want to interrupt while you two were breaking in the new act."

"But I feel terribly," says Lucinda.

"She's had good care, Lu, and Lizzie's right, we couldn't have dropped everything, or we'd never have gotten more bookings in the New Year," Billy says.

"She'll get her strength back in no time," Lizzie says, "And having you here just now is the best medicine, I can tell by looking at her."

"Need a hand putting that star on top?" Billy drops to the floor on all fours and points to his back. Lucinda giggles and steps up onto his makeshift stepstool, and reaches the top of the tree with ease.

"Perfect," Lizzie says. "The girls will be delighted when they come downstairs tomorrow morning. I'll go and check on them, and wish you a good night."

"Good night, Lizzie, and thank you for everything," Lucinda reaches for her friend and kisses her cheek. "I'll see to putting Norma to bed." She sits on the sofa and lets out a sigh of contentment. "Isn't it a treat to spend some time in a real house?"

Billy pokes a hissing log with a fire iron. "Beats the heck out of another night in a hotel," he says, and then he flops onto the other end of the sofa.

"I don't miss sharing the facilities."

"Or the diner meals. Don't miss washing my socks in the tiny sink in the hotel room, either."

"If there is a sink in the room," Lucinda laughs.

They sit in silence for a while, watching the fire. From the shadows in the armchair comes the gentle sound of Norma's steady breathing.

"I do miss one thing," Lucinda says, speaking just above a whisper, "And I never thought I'd say it, given how frightened I was a month ago, but I do miss the footlights, the applause. The excitement."

She looks over at him, and he studies the play of firelight on her face.

"There's one thing I miss more than any of that," he says in a low voice. Lucinda tilts her head and raises her eyebrows. "Kissing you in the wings." And he moves in close and kisses her. Then he takes her in his arms and he kisses her again.

CHAPTER TWENTY

Moving Picture

The laughs have built steadily from the start of the picture as Fatty and Al move from one silly situation to the next. Fatty puts on a tent-shaped dress to wear to the waiters' ball. He primps and flirts and bats his eyelashes, and Lucinda is sure she has never seen Billy laugh so hard. Throughout the film, in the safety of the darkened theatre, his hand has kept hers warm. Occasionally his thumb traces a circle on her palm, leaving her grateful she's sitting, else her knees might give out.

Now the two comedians are in the restaurant kitchen. Al grabs a broom and swats Fatty. Fatty picks up his own broom and hits Al. Beside her, Billy sits up straight. The theatre organist changes key and launches into "The Anvil Chorus," and the fellows onscreen are hitting each other in tempo. Billy's grip on her hand tightens and he draws a sharp breath. Lucinda watches his face in the flickering light of the screen; the muscles of his jaw are tight and he is no longer smiling, despite the shouts of laughter from the crowd around them.

"Dammit," he mutters just loudly enough.

"What's wrong?" she asks, but he hasn't heard her. He is watching the screen, frowning with his head slightly bowed and his fists clenched on the armrests of his chair.

The two-reeler ends to applause and boffo laughs, and as the lights come up Billy turns to her with a grim set to his jaw.

"Lu, do you mind if we leave now?" His voice is tight.

"And miss the feature film?"

"I'm sorry, but I can't stay. Maybe we can see *Intolerance* another time."

"Of course," she says, and he grabs their coats, takes her by the arm, and they make their way across the row of seats and up the aisle to the lobby.

"Billy, what's wrong? Are you all right?"

He helps her with her coat and shrugs his arms into his own.

"The bastard stole our gag," he says. "Sorry, Lu, I shouldn't swear. But *dammit.*"

"What do you mean, he stole your gag?"

"Arbuckle. He stole the Anvil Chorus gag from me and Pop. He must have seen us do it when we played the Palace in New York last year."

Billy holds the door open for her and Lucinda blinks at the daylight.

"I don't suppose there's much you can do about it, other than take it as a compliment," Lucinda says. "I mean, you do it all the time, parody the acts you admire."

"True," he says, "But it stinks when you see it on the big-screen and everyone is laughing, thinking it's Fatty's gag."

A trolley rumbles past, then a steady stream of automobiles honking their horns. There has been a wedding at the cathedral nearby, and the honking horns will go on for a while.

"Let's stop for coffee," Lucinda says, and they step into

[114]

the steamy warmth and quiet of a diner. "Meals 25 cents," reads a sign on the wall above their table. Condensation on the window blurs the view of the street.

"I wish I'd seen you do the Anvil Chorus gag," Lucinda says. "I'll bet you and your father were a whole lot funnier than Fatty and Al."

"We got some good laughs with that one," Billy says, and his eyes take on a distant look. Lucinda casts around for the right words to bring him back.

"Do you ever think about going into motion pictures? They say it's the next big thing."

Billy shakes his head as the waitress puts steaming cups of coffee on the table. "I'm not so sure about that. My Pop says it's a passing fad." He drops two sugar cubes into his cup.

"You'd be every bit as funny as Fatty," Lucinda says. "More so, even."

Billy allows a smile. "You know, Pop once refused a movie offer from William Randolph Hearst."

"Billy! Is this true?" Lucinda drops her spoon on the table with a clatter.

"Sure it is," Billy says. "Hearst offered us a series based on a comic strip. 1912, I think; I'd have been sixteen years old or so. Pop said no."

"Why on earth did he do that?"

"He said to Hearst, 'the Three Pascoes work for years perfecting our act, and you want to put us on a dirty bed-sheet for a nickel a head?' Hearst was furious. He thought we'd be the perfect knockabout act for his movies. He was probably right."

"Your father sounds like quite a character."

"He's that, all right," Billy says with a shrug.

"Maybe somebody will ask you again."

"Ask me about what, movies?"

"You're funnier than all of them put together, Billy," Lucinda says, and she reaches across the table and touches his hand. He looks for a moment at her, then he digs in his pocket and leaves some change on the table.

"Maybe someday," he says.

CHAPTER TWENTY-ONE

Snow Angels

CHRISTMAS WISHES TO MY DEAR FAMILY STOP AM WELL
AND THINKING HAPPY THOUGHTS OF MY DARLING LIZZIE
STOP LOVE TO LITTLE SNOW ANGELS WHOSE DADDY
THINKS OF THEM EVERY DAY STOP YOURS ALWAYS DAVID

Billy kneels and ties little Constance's bootlaces while
Lucinda helps Natalie button her coat.

"Uncle Billy, will you carry me?" Constance puts her
hands around his neck for balance.

"We haven't even stepped outside, Connie," he says as
he twists a double-bow in place. A crease appears between
the little girl's eyebrows.

"But you know I'll need you to carry me *outside*, so you
might as well start by carrying me *inside*."

Billy keeps as serious a face as Constance and nods his
head.

"Well, you're right about that," he says, and he offers her
the palm of his hand to stand on, then as he straightens to
his feet he lifts her elevator-style to his shoulder. There is
a leaping sensation in back of Lucinda's throat at the sight
of his ease with the child.

"Here's a Thermos of hot chocolate and some cookies,"
Norma says as she hands Lucinda a string bag. "Have fun

with the new toboggan, girls. Maybe later we'll sing some more."

"You look a little better today," Lucinda says, looking up at Norma. "There's colour in your cheeks."

"It's been such a happy Christmas. Having you and Billy and Myra here has been wonderful."

"I hate the thought of leaving you tomorrow."

"You know I'll be fine, Lucinda, and you've only got this afternoon before packing up, so let's not waste any of it being sad. Go and have some fun."

Norma kisses her on the cheek and then Natalie is tugging at her hand to go out the door. Billy is already on his way down the street, pulling the toboggan with Constance perched on his shoulders.

"Let's ride behind them," Lucinda whispers, and Natalie claps her hands in delight and runs after Billy. The two of them land giggling on the toboggan, and Billy barely breaks his stride as he pulls them through the snow.

*

"Time for bed, girls. Say good night to our guests and we'll all get up early in the morning to see them off." Lizzie ushers her daughters into the living-room.

"Where are they going in the morning?" Constance yawns and rubs her eyes.

"Remember what Mummy told us? They're going away to troupe," Natalie says.

"Where's Troupe?"

"It's a place where you sing and dance on a stage in front of lots of people, silly."

Constance's eyes widen and her bow-mouth turns down at the corners.

"But who will take us tobogganing?"

"We'll have plenty of time for tobogganing, dear," Lizzie says, smiling down at her daughter. "Why don't you give everyone a hug and a kiss, and I'll read you a story upstairs."

Natalie pulls Constance by the hand and leads her around the room for their good-nights. When they reach Billy, Constance climbs up on his lap.

"I don't want you to go away," she says, and she buries her face in his neck. He breathes in the sweet scent of her damp curls and gives Lucinda a pleading look.

"Will you come back, Uncle Billy?" Natalie stares at him with huge, unblinking eyes, and he holds out his free hand and pulls her up on his lap.

"I'll come back just as soon as I can," he says. "How about I read you your bedtime story tonight?" and he stands up with a girl in each arm and carries them upstairs with Lizzie close behind.

"See you in the morning, girls," Lucinda calls after them.

"Don't let the bedbugs bite," Myra adds. Her hands are busy with a red scarf and flying knitting needles. "Cutie-pies, those two, and they've got Billy wrapped around their little fingers." Her needles slow down a moment while she looks toward the staircase. "They're not the only ones missing their father this Christmas," she says quietly.

"They'll miss Billy," Norma says.

"He'll miss them, too," Lucinda says with a sigh.

"You got your trunk packed, Lucinda?" Myra asks.

"Just about," Lucinda says. "Thank you for having it sent from Muskoka, I'm glad of the extra space."

"Well, it's easier than lugging around two or three suitcases, and besides, you'll be gone a lot longer this time."

"I'm sure I have room if you'd like to pack anything of yours in it, Mrs. Pascoe."

Myra peers at her over her glasses and puts down her knitting.

"I won't be coming with you, at least not for now. I'm staying here until your sister's feeling better."

Lucinda stares at her, then at Norma.

"I tried to tell her I'll be all right," Norma says.

"You and Lizzie have your hands full with those little girls, and their father overseas until who-knows-when. I plan to stay here until you're right as rain, Norma, and I won't hear an argument."

"But that means ... I mean, Billy and I ..."

"That's right, Lucinda, you and Billy will have to manage without me," Myra says as she resumes knitting. "If anyone asks, you already had your twenty-first birthday last summer. Not that anyone'll be asking. Don't you worry, Billy will take good care of you."

Norma and Lucinda exchange a glance as the finality of Myra's words ends the discussion.

*

"I forgot to pack those new song sheets," Lucinda whispers from her bed.

"Don't worry, I've put them on the table by the front door," Norma says. "I won't let you forget them. Do you have enough stockings?"

"Yes, I bought some when Lizzie and I went shopping on

Thursday. I bought extra, just in case. And two more pairs of dance slippers; ribbon, too."

"I can't wait to see the act," Norma says. "Your reviews have been wonderful. Are you enjoying it?"

"I am now," Lucinda says, "But I was terrified the first couple of weeks. It felt as though I might slip through the floorboards at any moment."

"Billy tells me you're doing a marvelous job, Lu. He says you're a real trouper."

"He does most of the work." Lucinda smiles in the dark. "He makes it easy for me."

There is a rustling of sheets as Norma moves in her bed.

"You trust him onstage, don't you?"

"I trust him with my life," Lucinda says with a quiet laugh.

"Do you love him?"

Lucinda opens her mouth to speak, then closes it again.

"It's more than just trust, isn't it?"

"Yes, I suppose you could say that," she says.

"Billy cares about you, Lu, but be careful. Don't make the same mistake as I did."

"You don't need to worry."

"You're my baby sister," Norma says, "I'll always worry. Now, go to sleep, you've got a busy day tomorrow. Syracuse is a long way away."

"Good night, dear Norma," Lucinda fights back the tears that threaten to spill onto her cheeks.

"Good night, Lu. Sleep well."

CHAPTER TWENTY-TWO

Travels

Billy stows his rucksack in the overhead rack, folds his overcoat and lays it on top, then sits on the seat across from Lucinda. The train is picking up speed, lurching along past the rail yard, the stone majesty of Union Station receding from view. It feels like old times, that sense of anticipation and excitement hanging in the air along with the steam and the shriek of the train's whistle; the newness of opening a show.

"I'm ready to get back on-stage," he says. "A week away is plenty."

Lucinda smiles and looks out the window. She has been quiet ever since they left the house on Brunswick Street, her face pale with faint shadows beneath her eyes.

"I've been thinking about a new finish," he says, and the truth of it is, he's been thinking of little else but the act for the past couple of days.

"Don't you like what we've got?" Lucinda asks.

"It's good, but I don't want it to get stale," he says. "The audience always knows when you let something go for too long."

"What do you have in mind?"

Billy sits forward and rests his elbows on his knees.

"I'm thinking you can end with *A Lovely Day* as always, or try one of your new songs if you like. You bring the audience to tears, but before they can applaud you start a cool-down, stretching your feet one after another. I go on bended knee to one side of you, and when I look up to see if you accept my proposal, I discover you've switched sides. You don't even know I'm there. So I run around to the other side and do it all over again, same result. You haven't even seen me."

"Will I notice you at some point?"

"Not before you notice there's something wrong with your shoe."

"Maybe a ribbon has come loose," Lucinda says.

"Perfect. You go down on one knee to tighten the ribbon, and I'm walking around in a circle; I've given up. Then—and we'll have to time this part perfectly—just as I walk toward you, you look up, still on bended knee, and our eyes lock ..."

Lucinda sits up on the edge of her seat and finishes his sentence.

"And you think I'm proposing to you!"

"Exactly! Then I react and pull a laugh out of the audience."

"And then you take me by the wrist and lead me offstage. Oh, Billy, it's brilliant!"

"You'll give it a try?" Billy is pleased to see Lucinda so animated.

"Yes, of course!"

"We'll walk through it Monday morning at the hall."

CHAPTER TWENTY-THREE

Son-of-a-gun

NOTICE TO PERFORMERS

*Don't say "slob" or "son-of-a-gun" or "hully-gee"on this
stage unless you want to be cancelled peremptorily.
Do not address anyone in the audience in this manner.
If you have not the ability to entertain Mr. Black's
audiences without risk of offending them, do the
best you can. Lack of talent will be less open to
censure than would an insult to a patron.*

Billy steps into the properties room, which has the familiar
look of countless other prop rooms he's made use of over
the years. There are kitchen chairs, a landscape painting
hanging on the wall next to a photo portrait of a severe-
looking woman in a black bonnet, and a dining table with
two smaller tables and a desk lamp stacked atop it. Draped
over an armchair there is a polar bear rug, and a bottomless
galvanized bucket hangs from a hook by the door. To one
side a barrel holds three brooms and two crutches.

"Harry Stanby, is that you?" Billy sets the barre pieces on
the floor and holds out his hand to the props manager who
is grinning around the cigarette between his lips.

"If it isn't Billy Pascoe!" he says, rheumy eyes peering

out from under bristly eyebrows. The two men shake hands and slap each other on their backs. "It's been a couple of years, hasn't it? Good to see you, boy."

"Good to see you, Harry. How's the house?"

"Busy as always, usually a full house. Sorry to hear about your old man; he's always the life of the party down at Jimmy's Tavern."

"Well, I guess the last time he was in a tavern he was a little too lively," Billy says. "Samuel Black thought so too. That's why you haven't seen us in a while. We haven't played Black's theatres in a couple of years."

"How's the new act breaking in? Word is your Miss Hart does a fine job. Here, let me see that."

"We've had a pretty good run, so far," Billy says as he crouches to clamp the barre together. "Some good reviews. Wait'll you hear Lucinda sing. There won't be a breath out of the audience."

"Is she a looker, Billy?"

Billy straightens. "She's pretty, yes," he says. "Why do you ask?"

Harry pushes the door shut. "Don't let her out of your sight, then, not while Bob Black is in the house," he says. "He's got a quick and nasty hand around the ingénues. Not much those poor girls can do when the theatre manager makes a pass."

"Thanks for the warning," Billy says. "Say, you got a coat tree in here we can use for our act?" He looks around at the props, tries to ignore the tightening of his jaw.

"I had one of the boys take it up earlier. They've already got the upright piano onstage; a couple of other acts will be using it, too. You'll close in One, will you?"

"We can do it in One, yes, as long as we've got the spread of the stage," Billy says.

"Just as well, the Flying Escalantes are billed to close. We'll set them up behind the curtain while you're on. It'll keep Mr. Black happy, too."

"Anything to keep Mr. Black happy." Billy rolls his eyes.

*

"We need to tighten up the timing when our eyes meet, Lu. Let's do it again. Start with your left foot stretch and count to three before changing."

Billy goes down on one knee to her right just as Lucinda looks at her left foot and stretches it. He sees that she is looking the other way and scurries behind her to the other side just as she turns to her right foot. Billy kneels again, sees that she is again looking the other way.

"Count it out as I walk behind you. Try seven."

He puts his hands in his pockets and walks toward stage left just as Lucinda notices her loosened ribbon. She kneels to fix it.

"... five, six, look up at me, seven. Good. Now, on eight, hold it a beat."

Lucinda and Billy both freeze, then he clasps his hands and looks away, suddenly bashful. Lucinda's eyes widen as he takes her by the wrist and she stands.

"Better?" she asks.

"Better, but not perfect. Let's do it again."

There is a wariness in his eyes she hasn't seen before onstage.

"This feels like rehearsal," she says as she resumes her position.

"Mmm, I guess you could say," he says. "Once more, look at your left foot and stretch ..."

"Pascoe!" A raspy voice cuts through the theatre, and they both look up to see a lone figure lumbering down the aisle, using his cane with flourish. He is dressed in a suit and spats and a bowler hat. The glint of spectacles catches the stage lights; to Lucinda he looks every bit the part of the intimidating Theatre Manager.

"It's Black," Billy mutters under his breath, the muscles of his jaw working.

"Careful, Billy," Lucinda whispers, and as she steps forward to the apron of the stage, Billy follows. "Good day, Mr. Black," she says.

"Mr. Black," Billy echoes.

"Miss Hart, is it?" Black removes his bowler to reveal luxuriant hair combed to one side. "I haven't seen you since you and your sister were girls. You're a young lady, now." His eyes are invisible behind the glare on his spectacles, and his smile is completely lacking in warmth. Lucinda is glad of the distance the orchestra pit puts between them. She can sense Billy bristling beside her.

"How do you do, sir," she says.

"The better for having seen you, my dear." Black turns his spectacles on Billy. "Long time, no see, Pascoe. You two have had some fair reviews, better than you and your old man. I'll be keeping a close eye on your act tonight. But don't let me keep you from rehearsing. I'll just make myself comfortable."

He leans his cane against an aisle seat and lowers himself

to the chair, resting his elbows on the armrests and cross-
ing his fingers, teepee style.

"Make *me* laugh, Pascoe," he growls, and Billy straightens his back as though readying to lunge across the orchestra pit and tackle him. He opens his mouth to speak, but
Lucinda rushes in before he can say anything.

"We've just finished rehearsing, sir," she says, "But thank
you for your interest."

She takes Billy by the arm and leads him offstage. She
is surprised to find herself shaking as though it were opening night. Billy's face is white with rage.

"I need some air," he mutters, and he disappears up the
stairs to the flies.

Lucinda turns to find the props manager looking up the
stairway after Billy.

"There's a fire escape upstairs. I wouldn't be surprised if
you'd find him sitting out there," he says.

"Thank you, Mr. Stanby," Lucinda says as she puts her
foot on the first step.

"Here, take this so's you don't catch cold." Mr. Stanby
hands her a prop blanket, and she dashes up the stairs.

*

Lucinda walks carefully with her hand on the railing. Far
below her the stage is divided four-across by curtains, and
various props are already being pushed into place by stage
hands. Three trapezes lie on the floor awaiting installation
by the Flying Escalantes. Lucinda pushes open the fire
door and steps outside, where the sudden rush of cold air
makes her cough.

Billy is sitting on the top step, smoking a cigarette.

"You shouldn't be out here, you'll catch cold," he says, but still he makes room for her on the fire escape. Lucinda sits down and drapes the blanket across their knees.

"He's a nasty piece of work, that Mr. Black," she says, and leaves unspoken the worry that Black could fire them at his whim.

"I'd slap the taste right out of his mouth if I could get within three feet of him."

"Which is why you're going to keep away from him."

"You stay clear, too," Billy says. "Stick with me, and if you can't, then find Mr. Stanby."

"Don't worry, I'll be fine," she says, at the same time giving an involuntary shudder at the memory of Black leering up at her from the aisle.

She looks down at the alleyway below where people are scurrying with their heads bent against the wind.

"It's not the first time I've found you outside in the cold," she says softly. Billy draws on his cigarette and looks at her. "Tonight's opening, it isn't just like any other Monday, is it?"

"Nope." Billy stubs his cigarette on the railing next to him.

"And that's why we'll make it our best show yet," she says.

A hint of a smile plays on his lips, and he flicks the cigarette butt into the air.

"Yep," he says, and they both watch the cigarette spiral to the alleyway below where it disappears in the snow.

CHAPTER TWENTY-FOUR

Black's Theatre

GRAND OPERA HOUSE
Monday Evening, January 1
BLACK'S VAUDEVILLE
7 BIG 7
BIG FEATURE ACTS

PRICES:
Lower Floor, 75¢; Balcony, 50¢; Gallery, 25¢; Box Seats, $2

PROGRAM
MAXWELL HOLDEN
Shadowgraphist
PASCOE & HART
Ballet Comedy Duo
THE HANAS
Novelty Roller Skating Act
PAUL LA CROIX & COMPANY
Comedy Hat Manipulators
8 GIRLS OF THE GOLDEN WEST
Big Scenic Instrumental Music Act
GILBERT "SPURS" ANDERSON
American Cow Boy
THE FLYING ESCALANTES
Trapeze Artists Extraordinaire

CHAPTER TWENTY-FIVE

Rescue

Billy lines his eye, glares at the mess he's made of it, and rubs it off.

"You'd think I was a leftie," he says as he tries again with the makeup stick.

"Take your time, Billy, you're rushing yourself." Beside him Lu is powdering her face.

"I can't help it, I need to get upstairs and check on the barre."

"I'm sure it's fine, Mr. Stanby has his eye on it. Here, let me do that. Sit still." Lucinda takes the makeup stick from him and holds Billy by the chin. "Close your eyes."

"I still want to check it," Billy says as she finishes his eye with a few deft strokes.

"If it makes you feel better, then I guess you should. But don't forget your mouth."

"Pardon?

"Your mouth." Lucinda holds out the carmine stick.

"Right. Thanks." Billy takes the carmine and rubs a small amount on his lips. Already he is standing crouched before the mirror, ready for flight.

"I'll only be gone a minute. Keep the door closed, and don't let anyone in. *Anyone.*"

"Don't worry, I won't." Lucinda picks up the Brown No. 7 and outlines her left eye as Billy closes the dressing room door behind him. She has never seen him like this before; tonight he is taut with nerves. She takes a deep breath, thinks through their new finish. Hums a scale, then an arpeggio. Soon she is singing full-voice, warming her upper register. Tonight she will sing her very best, she will help Billy show Mr. Black what Pascoe & Hart are capable of. She draws a deep breath for her next arpeggio and in that instant there is a faint tapping at the door. She holds her breath and freezes, holding aloft the Brown No. 7.

There is a cough, then a familiar rasping voice.

"Miss Hart."

It's Black. Lucinda turns and faces the door, her pulse racing in her ears.

"Miss Hart, are you in there?"

She looks around for something to protect herself. The nearest thing is Billy's ukulele, hanging by a strap on a hook on the wall. Slowly she reaches for it, staring all the while at the door.

"I just want to wish you well, Miss Hart. I look forward to seeing *you* tonight."

There is the sound of receding footsteps punctuated by the tapping of a cane, barely discernible over the thudding of her heart. Lucinda loosens her grip on the neck of Billy's uke, and in spite of herself, she gives a shaky laugh at the thought of using it in self-defence. The strings chime softly in her trembling hands.

*

Billy is standing on the other side of the barre with an exaggerated look of expectancy. *What is he waiting for?*

[134]

He peers at her once, places his hands on his hips and peers again. Stares at the audience, perplexed. There is a titter from beyond the footlights that turns into a chuckle as he pulls Lucinda's arm forward and smacks himself in the forehead with the back of her hand. *The kick! Yes, the kick.* While he stumbles groggily she swings her leg back with extra force and sends him skittering forward, clutching his rear end. The guffaw is a relief. Billy gives her a beat, then two more to recover, his eyes watchful.

Her near-miss with Black has thrown her concentration. It's not so much the flapping bird in her chest as a fogginess that has set in, an unfamiliar dullness.

Snap out of it.

"Where d'you suppose he's sitting?" she'd asked Billy as they waited to go on, and he sneaked a look through the peephole in the curtain.

"Stage right box seat, alone," Billy said, just as the orchestra started up their introduction. "Knock 'em dead," he said as she took her first steps onstage, and that's when the fog settled. She took her place at the barre and rested her hand on it, and then her mind went blank.

For a moment she stopped breathing and her body stiffened. Without moving her head she cast her eyes to Billy in the wings. Immediately he went down into a plié with his arm in a perfect arc over his head, and in that instant she knew two things: *Pliés, yes.* Also, she had never seen a man move with such grace. *Billy could be a dancer*, she thought, as she forced her knees to bend and found her rhythm.

They have moved on from the kick in the pants.

"Forget about him," Billy whispers at one point. And, "Let's have some fun," at another. He grabs his ukulele from the top of the piano and hops up on top of it, and the pianist quickly switches to *Down By the Old Mill Stream*. At the sight of Billy's uke, the fog begins to lift.

*

Billy moves them from one gag to another seamlessly, directed by the response from the audience. Occasionally he sneaks a look in Black's direction, to make sure he's taking in the laughter. Early in the act, Black sits with his arms folded and a smug set to his flabby jaw—"Make *me* laugh, Pascoe"—and soon after, as the audience shouts and hollers their appreciation, he is pointedly looking away from the stage through his opera glasses, no doubt checking out some unfortunate girl in the gallery. Billy goes big on his aerial cartwheels, and when he lands on his ass the laughter and applause that follows is the loudest he's heard in a long time. He jumps to his feet and places his hand to his ear, guiding their attention to Lucinda's soaring soprano.

When you come to the end of a Perfect Day
And you sit alone with your thought ...

He knows she is frightened. He also knows she has no idea how her voice affects him.

While the chimes ring out with a carol gay
For the joy the day has brought ...

And he knows that at times like this her stage fright is such that the only thing keeping her from toppling to the floor is the notes she is singing.

Do you think what the end of a Perfect Day
Can mean to a tired heart?

The expressions that travel across her face as she sings remind him of the wind ruffling the surface of the lake. Billy is grateful to be on bended knee, as he's not sure he could stand at the moment.

When the sun goes down with a flaming ray
And the dear friends have to part.

The final note is pulling her upward, and he follows, along with nearly everyone in the hall. Everyone but Black, that is. From the corner of his eye, Billy sees him haul his hulking form up from his seat and lumber toward the door.

Billy moves swiftly, positioning himself to propose on Lucinda's left side as she stretches her right foot. Then he changes sides, and as the audience laughs, Black pauses and turns to watch. Billy plays up his moroseness as he shuffles to one side—*five, six, seven.* He takes one last hopeless glance at his love and finds her on bended knee gazing up at him. Billy clasps his hands, twists away from her shyly, and thumps at his heart.

"This is so sudden," he cries in a squeaky falsetto, and the audience is theirs. Billy helps her to her feet. Lucinda gives him a tentative smile, and he hoists her across his shoulders and strides offstage to the golden sound of belly laughs.

Black wouldn't dare fire them now.

*

"Thanks for rescuing me," Lucinda says as she begins to smudge her lip rouge. Billy takes her face in his hands and kisses her once and then again, and they kiss for what seems a very long time.

"Billy!" Mr. Stanby steps around from behind the curtain. "Keep moving!"

Lucinda gives his cheek a quick and expert going-over with the boot-black, and he smacks his hands together and falls to the floor. Lucinda counts five beats and saunters onstage with her hands behind her back, casting her eye to the box at stage right, then at Billy. She lifts her chin and keeps going, and the audience cheers and claps.

Offstage, fuelled by adrenaline, Billy is hopping, springing silently higher and higher as she makes her deliberate way across the stage. When finally she reaches stage left, she gives a little wave to the audience and disappears into the wings. Billy sprints to mid-stage, stops, and gives a fevered glare to the audience. He looks around wildly for her, and then he stumbles to stage left, finishing with a running forward flip into the wings.

Bows: Tonight there are five. Each time they bow, Billy sneaks a look up at the empty box at stage right, a tiny smile on his face.

CHAPTER TWENTY-SIX

Vaudeville Talent Review

W.R. MCCALLUM, AGENT

No. 8—*Digby Bell.* Time: 17 min. All in One. The title of his monologue is new, but that is all. He now uses a tough gallery boy recitation, in place of the old baseball piece. In this he makes good for the only time during the act.

No. 9—*Pascoe & Hart.* Time: 15 min. Can close in One. Two-act: young woman, young man. Some nice ballet by the girl, also some fine soprano singing. Really good comedy by the boy as well as superb acrobatics. Very good small act, goes well here.

CHAPTER TWENTY-SEVEN

Closing Night at Black's

Of closing night at Black's, Billy recalls building the gags, one sequence after another, and it's beautiful, just like the old days with the Three Pascoes when his mother played them on with her saxophone and he and Pop did their business chasing and swatting with brooms, flying on and off the table in a series of perfect flips and pratfalls. To close, Billy swung his basketball on a rubber rope ever closer to Pop, who was shaving his neck with a straight razor, and when he knocked the hat off his head the audience screamed their laughter and terror, and it was pure, comic dance.

Tonight, closing night, Billy flips and falls around a delicate ballerina who captivates him with her grace and beauty, and mesmerizes everyone within range with her voice (although she still does not know this), and his heartache only makes her moment of realization all the sweeter as they fall in love and leave the stage together to boffo laughs and cheers.

He recalls the feel of her hand in his as he stood for her curtsy, the arch of her neck and the way the spotlight illuminated her blue eyes.

And he recalls leaving her for a moment, just a moment,

when halfway down the stairs he decided to return to the wings and relieve the stage manager of the prop barre.

*

"I'll be right back," Billy calls, "Won't take a minute."

"All right," Lucinda says, and she watches him take the stairs three at a time. Billy is always charged and restless following a performance, whereas she would rather sit quietly and come back to herself. She will take advantage of a few solitary minutes in the dressing room, and simply breathe.

She turns and continues down the steel stairway, carefully placing one foot after another so as not to slip in her ballet shoes.

She feels Mr. Black coming before she hears him. The stairs bounce with the rhythm of heavy footfall, then the clatter of a walking-stick banging against the railing.

"Miss Hart," comes his raspy voice. Without turning to look behind her, Lucinda quickens her pace, her fingertips tingling with growing panic.

"Miss Hart, I'm speaking to you."

She is near the bottom of the staircase when she slips and falls, and before she can stand he is upon her, grabbing her by the arm.

"Allow me," he says, and he twists her arm behind her and pushes her through the nearest doorway and slams it shut. In the darkness she trips over something, a chair, perhaps, and when she cries out a sweaty hand slaps across her mouth.

[142]

"Keep quiet, you little whore, or you and Pascoe'll never work the Big Time again," he hisses.

His breath is foul with whiskey and liverwurst and he shoves her against a wall, whimpering and facing away from him with her cheek pressed against plaster. One clammy hand is across her mouth and the other is reaching under her tutu when there is a click and light floods what turns out to be the properties room. Within her range of vision there is a polar bear, draped across a chair, staring at her with frozen, glass eyes.

"Come on, now, Mr. Black, you don't want to hurt the girl, do you."

A statement, not a question, delivered in a low, even voice by Mr. Stanby.

"Let's you and me take a walk, sir, and find you a cup of coffee."

Black wheezes in her ear and releases her with a shove and a grunt, and lurches toward the door. Lucinda stands rigid for a moment, then turns to see Mr. Stanby at the doorway with one hand on a baseball bat and the other across Billy's chest, restraining him.

"Steady, boy, she needs you most," Stanby says to Billy, all the while keeping his eyes on Black, and Lucinda can see that it takes all of Billy's will for him not to lunge at Black and kill him.

*

Of closing night at Black's, Billy recalls a boiling fury that just about took the top of his head off as Black stumbled past, and Stanby held Billy back from committing murder.

"Steady, boy, she needs you most."

Stanby's words had brought him back to Lucinda, and as Stanby let him go and grabbed Black and quickly and forcefully walked him away, Billy turned to see her face, white and uncomprehending, in the moment that her legs gave out and she sank to the floor, gasping.

"Billy, oh, B-Bil ..." Her teeth were chattering and she could say no more, her hands cold as ice as he knelt beside her and wrapped himself around her.

*

All of this Billy recalls as he arranges his pillow and a blanket on the floor of Lucinda's hotel room, beneath the window and to the side of the small, enamel sink. Next to him, beneath the window, the ornate and gilded radiator makes undignified noises as hot water rushes through it.

In spite of her reassurances and her insistence that he return to his own room, he has been sitting on the chair by her bed for the last hour, watching her toss and turn and finally settle into some sort of sleep. He will never leave her alone again.

Billy lies on the floor and pulls the blanket up under his chin. The radiator gives him warmth but little comfort as he stares at the light from a nearby street lamp slanting across the ceiling.

He rolls onto his side and allows his thoughts to travel through their act, as he often does in the last moments before sleep takes him: Lucinda walking onstage before him; his entrance with the broom, sweeping here and there, gauging the audience for laughs; Lucinda's outstretched hand smacking his nose, and her foot kicking his rear end.

There is a faint rustling of bed sheets beside him, and his eyes fly open to see one small foot, then another, followed by the white cloud of her nightie as she drops to the floor and slips under his blanket, where she curls up in his arms. As her breathing finds its rhythm, Billy tightens his hold on her. He lies awake until eventually the street lamp gives way to the watery light of dawn.

CHAPTER TWENTY-EIGHT

Pillow Talk

"It's Rogers. Mr. and Mrs. W. Rogers," Billy says, tugging the brim of his hat a little lower over his eyes. Lucinda feels a blush rising on her cheeks, and turns away from the concierge's inquisitive eyes. Stacked behind them are their packing trunks, sure giveaways to their vaudevillian lives.

"Would that be Mr. Will Rogers, sir?" the concierge asks, as he consults his list.

"Call me Bill," Billy says, and he slides his eyes over to her and winks.

"Always a pleasure to serve the entertainment world's finest, Mr. Rogers. The Hudson Theatre is only half a block from here, and we provide a taxi service in the event of inclement weather." The concierge offers Lucinda a smile. "The bellboy will show you to your room. I'll have your trunks sent up promptly."

*

"Thank you, good man," Billy says as he hands the bellboy some change. He turns to Lucinda and says with a slight bow, "After you, Mrs. Rogers."

Lucinda bites her lip and is about to step through the door to their room when Billy sweeps her up in his arms.

"I nearly forgot," he says, and he carries her over the

threshold into their sunlit room. There is the usual sink with a wardrobe closet to one side of it, two chairs and a small table by the window, and in the middle of the room, impossible to ignore, there is a four-poster double bed. Billy pauses inside the door and they both look at it. Lucinda clears her throat and eases herself from Billy's arms.

"It isn't quite proper, is it?" she says. "Mr. Rogers."

"Well, I won't leave you on your own, and besides, I'm sleeping on the floor."

"That isn't proper, either, Billy."

"We agreed we'd try this, just for this week we're in Union Hill," Billy says, as he shrugs off his woolen coat and unwinds his scarf.

"But what if someone discovers us?"

"No-one will discover us." Billy opens the wardrobe and is greeted by a whiff of cedar. "I'm not leaving you alone, and that's final."

Lucinda sits on the nearest chair and looks out the window, anything to avoid looking at the bed. When she wakes in the night with the feel of Black's hand on her mouth and his breath in her ear, and her pulse roars in her ears as she tries to scream but can't, the only thing that calms her is knowing Billy is near.

"He thinks you're Will Rogers," Lucinda says, suddenly overcome with giggles.

"I never said I was Will," Billy says. "I'm Will's kid brother, Bill." He draws himself up to his full five-foot-six and assumes a bow-legged cowboy stance that sends him toppling to the floor with a crash.

"Billy, shh! What will they think downstairs?"

"They'll think we're doing what every married couple

does," Billy says as he pulls himself to his feet and throws himself on the bed with his hands folded behind his head. "Even midday." He gives her a sly look from the corner of his eye. "You know, arguing over where to eat lunch."

Lucinda looks at her hands.

"It still isn't proper, you know."

Billy sits up and swings his legs over the side of the bed, facing her.

"What would make it proper?" he asks.

"What do you mean?"

"I mean, what would make it proper for us to share a room, short of being Mr. and Mrs. W. Rogers?"

"Well, I suppose if we were married, but ..."

"Then we'll marry."

And he is on one knee before her with his hands across his heart, just like the close of their act.

"Marry me, Lu," he says, fixing his dark, unblinking eyes on her. Lucinda looks at a spot on the wall behind him, and then looks at him again. His face still and waiting, impossible to read, just as it is on-stage. She fights the urge to laugh, and instead she touches his cheek.

"You'd do that for me, wouldn't you, Billy."

"Is that a yes?"

"It's a ..." Lucinda searches for the right words. "It's a thank you," she says, and he nods and looks away.

*

Much later, as she lies alone on the enormous bed watching the play of moonlight splashed across the wall, she listens to the soft sound of Billy's breathing. He is curled on a pile of blankets on the floor by the wardrobe, having finally accepted her offer of a pillow, although not without resistance. The box spring creaks once as she sits and again as her feet find the floor.

"What ..." Billy sits up in the shadows. Lucinda holds out her hand, palm-up.

"Do you want your pillow back?" His voice is thick with sleep. Lucinda takes the pillow, and holds out her hand again.

"Bring yours, too," she says, and she clutches the pillow as though to still the fluttering in her chest.

He rubs his hands across his face and looks up at her, his eyes jewels in the darkness.

Slowly he stands.

"Dreaming, I'm dreaming," he mumbles.

Lucinda opens her mouth to say no, he's not dreaming and neither is she, but no sound comes forth. Instead she steps closer to him, and as he reaches for her the pillow stops him touching her. Without taking his eyes off her, Billy gently pulls it from her grip and tosses it onto the bed. His hands slip around Lucinda's waist and he draws her to him and kisses her, and it is nothing like their stolen kisses in the wings, part fun but also work, an audience waiting beyond the footlights and the two of them jittery with adrenaline.

They breathe together and his fingers catch the moonlight in her hair. Lucinda smiles in the dark, for the moment is theirs alone.

CHAPTER TWENTY-NINE

Audition

Lucinda awakens to the sight of Billy lying beside her with his eyes closed and his mouth slightly opened. With his face in repose, the morning light catches his sculpted cheekbones and the curl of his eyelashes, a sight she will never tire of; one she has quickly grown accustomed to.

She slips out of bed and pulls her shawl around her shoulders, and pads over to the sink where she splashes some water on her face. The cold helps waken her more fully, and as she looks around the room something white catches her eye, an envelope fallen on the floor in the night. She picks it up and takes it over to the chair by the window for better light. Written across the back of the envelope in an elegant hand is *Miss Lucinda Hart*. Quietly she opens it, so as not to waken Billy.

> *Cleary's Hotel*
> *Union Hill, New Jersey*
> *22 January 1917*

My Dear Miss Hart,

Tonight I had the distinct pleasure of hearing you sing at the Hudson Theatre. I wish to commend you on your lovely soprano and impressive range, which puts you in the rarified ranks of coloratura. You were recommended to me by

the talent agent Mr. W.R. McCallum, and I must agree with
him entirely that you have a fine voice; indeed, exceptional.

I am holding auditions for the New York Operetta Soci-
ety's spring production of the Gilbert and Sullivan oper-
etta, Pirates of Penzance. Would you consider auditioning
for the role of Mabel? Rehearsals will commence early in
March and the performances will occur mid-May. I pro-
pose hearing you sing the aria "Poor Wand'ring One" to
test your vocal range and stamina. I have taken the liber-
ty of leaving the score with Mr. Solomon, the pianist at the
Hudson Theatre.

I may be reached at the above address until Thursday
midday, when I will return to New York City. I do plan to
attend your Wednesday evening performance.

I am,
Yours most respectfully,
Maestro Simon Caulfield
(Music Director, New York Operetta Society)

Lucinda's hands tremble as she folds the letter and looks
out the window. On the telegraph pole near her a crow settles, flapping its wings once for balance, then angling its
head in quick motions as it looks around. Automobiles and
delivery wagons make their way along the street below, but
she does not take in the sight of them.

*

"It must have fallen out of my coat pocket," Billy says as
she hands him the letter. "One of the ushers gave to it me

on our way out of the theatre last night." He reads the letter, folds it, and hands it back to her.

"You have to do it," he says.

"Oh, I don't know."

"What don't you know?" Billy's eyes widen. "There's a famous maestro telling you he thinks you have a fine voice, indeed *exceptional*," he raises his eyebrows and affects a nasal British accent. "And he wants you to audition for him. Honestly, Lu, what have you got to lose?"

"What about the act? What about Pascoe & Hart?" Lucinda twists the fringe of her shawl in her fingers. *What about us?* The words hang unspoken in the air.

Billy looks at the letter folded on her lap. Blinks once, then again.

"We'll cross that bridge when we get to it. It's an option, Lu, and an opportunity for someone important to hear you sing. What'd he call you, a colorata? Rare as hen's teeth, you coloratas."

"It's *coloratura*," she says with a reluctant smile. "It means high soprano."

"Well, then, you'll take that coloratura down to the theatre this morning and have a look at *Poor Wand'ring One*. Mr. Solomon probably already knows it."

"I suppose it can't hurt," she says doubtfully.

"You still don't know, do you?" Billy shakes his head and fixes his gaze on her. "You don't know what a voice you have."

Lucinda's face warms with a flush and she's not at all certain if it's because of Billy's words or his steady gaze.

CHAPTER THIRTY

Hudson Evening Register

Billy Pascoe, once billed as The Human Mop, must be thanking his lucky stars to have found someone unwilling to toss him around the stage. Boffo Billy assists the lovely Lucinda Hart at the Paramount Theater this week, with few worries about being tossed about as he was as a young lad headlining for the Three Pascoes. That he is an excruciatingly funny young man will be granted by anyone who sees him. Boffo Billy indulges in some clever parody and eye-popping acrobatics, which is balanced by Miss Hart's graceful dancing and her singing. Miss Hart's soaring treble is not to be underestimated; she possesses a voice of unusual clarity and range. When an encore is demanded it is hoped the two of them will provide an enthusiastic audience with more laughter and song.

CHAPTER THIRTY-ONE

Poor Wand'ring One

"I'm singing it this afternoon," Lucinda says evenly as she dusts a final puff of powder on her forehead.

"What, for the matinee?" Billy stops tying his slap-shoe and looks at her, a slight frown creasing his brow.

"You're the one who says the audience always knows when something's getting stale. I'm tired of *A Perfect Day*, and I want to try it."

"You sure about that, Lu? I mean, you've only just learned it."

"Yes, I'm sure. Maestro Caulfield said in his letter that he'd be in the audience tonight. Let's treat this afternoon as a rehearsal. You won't need to do much, and ..."

"Don't you worry about me," Billy says. Already he is thinking ahead, recalling Lucinda's rehearsal with Mr. Solomon, the high points and the drama of *Poor Wand'ring One*. "As long as you're sure."

"Please don't try to talk me out of it, Billy." Her eyes hold a steely calm.

He won't need to do much; probably he'll just sit atop the piano and react. Lucinda's singing will take care of the rest.

"I wouldn't dream of talking you out of it, Lu. I may even try a few new things, myself."

Billy gives his shoelace a final tug. He pushes aside

the thought that this evening's performance might be the beginning of the end of Pascoe & Hart.

*

They have finished the business with the pliés, and now Lucinda is reaching forward. As her hand approaches, Billy leans in closer than usual to see what she is doing. This time her hand slaps him in the nose audibly; there is nothing staged about it. Billy staggers backward, stumbling faster and faster out of control until he trips and falls into a backward roll and onto his feet again, still staggering into yet another backward roll, and comes to an abrupt stop with his back against the piano and his feet splayed in front of him at right angles. Lucinda continues calmly with her stretches, and as Billy gives a startled look over the footlights, the audience shouts with laughter.

He stands and returns to the barre, peers cautiously and ducks when her hand comes forward. He thinks he's cleared it, only to stroll around behind her and have her back-kick land square in the seat of his pants. Billy hops forward clutching his rear end, and is suddenly distracted by the new piece the accompanist is playing. He saunters over and watches from behind Mr. Solomon's shoulder, nodding appreciatively. He points at the page and raises his eyebrows at Mr. Solomon, who nods his head. Billy reaches carefully to turn the page, which becomes stuck between his fingers like flypaper.

What no-one in the hall but the two of them knows is that Billy has pointed to a repeat section, something Mr. Solomon can play in his sleep, and something the two of them

[158]

arranged before the show started. What everyone sees is Mr. Solomon's growing irritation and Billy's panic as he struggles to turn the page, and succeeds in covering the two of them with a cascade of music sheets as they unfold like an accordion and spread all over Mr. Solomon's lap and onto the floor.

Billy tries everything to un-stick the pages from between his fingers, and winds up dashing around the stage as though being chased by a paper serpent. Meanwhile, Lucinda continues her work at the barre with her head turned away from the audience to conceal the giggles that threaten to overtake her.

As a last resort, Billy hurls himself into his aerial cartwheels, and the music sheets flow along with him like a giant ribbon caught in the wind. Finally he lands on his rump on top of the music. He looks first at one empty hand, then at the other. Success! He glances toward the piano, wipes his forehead—*phew*—and clambers to his feet. The sheets are, of course, stuck to the seat of his pants, the paper serpent getting the last and boffo laugh. Billy jumps as though bitten, tears himself free, and leaps to safety on the piano lid as Mr. Solomon launches into the opening chords of *Poor Wand'ring One*.

*

Poor wand'ring one!
Though thou hast surely strayed,
Take heart of grace,
Thy steps retrace,
Poor wand'ring one!

The change in the air is instant as the audience quietens to the sound of Lucinda's voice.

Poor wand'ring one!
If such a love as mine
Can help thee find
Thy peace of mind—

And there she pauses, holding a note as clear and sleek as the chiming of a bell.

Billy can do no more than listen from his perch on top of the piano, where he sits cross-legged and entranced.

Why, take it, it is thine!

Mr. Solomon plays through the chorus, embellishing here and there while Lucinda gazes out at the audience. No matter where she turns her head, it seems the stage lights catch perfection in the contours of her face. At tonight's show Billy may do some business with the song, but for now he will sit still and absorb the purity of Lucinda's voice.

Take heart, fair days will shine;
Take any heart—take mine!

She holds the highest note Billy has ever heard her utter, for the longest time imaginable, before allowing it to cascade first in a trickle, then in a tumble to the final cadence.

And with her finish, Billy leads the applause, clapping wildly and toppling off the piano with the force of it. After he rights himself, he simply takes her by the hand and steps

back. She raises her eyebrows and he nods, and she dips
into a curtsy to thunderous applause.

*

Sleep will come eventually, she knows, but not before the
evening's performance has played itself in her mind a dozen
times; and even at that, once sleep finally takes her, she will
only just float beneath the surface of wakefulness. But she
does not mind.

It was the ease with which she sang the final caden-
za, her controlled fall from high to low, and the strength
behind that ease that finally convinced her that they're
right, Norma, Billy, Myra, and even Maestro Caulfield.
She can do this, she can at least try to do justice to the
songs she dreams of singing before an audience.

Again Billy gave her the performance. He built up the
gags only to the point where she would shine the brightest
of the act, and then he handed her the bows, refusing to take
one himself. When the single red rose landed at her feet,
he'd been the one to reach for it and hold it out to her, and
as he stood so near she saw it in his eyes, a deep sadness.

She knew in that moment that he was prepared to let
her go.

CHAPTER THIRTY-TWO

Sister Act

336 Brunswick, Toronto
5 February 1917

Darling Lu,

I read with great pride and a full heart your description of Maestro Caulfield's audition request, also of your performance the day after receiving his request, and the maestro's subsequent offer of the role of Mabel. What wonderful and exciting news!

Performing a song so new to your repertoire—indeed the day after learning it—takes a sort of courage which only comes with maturity, and my dear, you have matured by at least a decade in the three months you and Billy have been working together.

You must feel no obligation to our Sister Act when considering your future. I have long been telling you that you are a singer of rare talents, and now you must believe me. And believe me, too, when I tell you how happy I am that this opportunity has come to you.

I have been enjoying my new life in Toronto more than you can imagine. Since I've been giving the two little Pike girls piano lessons, some of the neighbouring families have requested my services, also to lead the children's choir at the Pikes' church. It's a quiet, peaceful life compared to the trouping we have been doing all these years, and I quite like it.

I have met a nice young man at the church who plays the organ beautifully. We've taken several walks together following the service where we have talked long into the afternoon comparing the music of J. S. Bach to some of our favourite parlour songs, and Lu, you wouldn't believe the influence Mr. Bach has had on the music you and I know so well!

All of this is my roundabout way of telling you, dear, that it seems the time has come for us to close the door on our Sister Act, which has brought us so far in life and has now pointed us both in new directions. I feel confident that you are ready to follow your new path, as am I.

Where this leaves Pascoe & Hart is not for me to say, but I am certain that the right choices for the both of you will reveal themselves in due course. I know Billy wants what's best for you; and you him. That sort of loyalty will always win out.

I send you my very best love, and warm greetings to Billy, whom Connie and Natalie talk about all the time.

With pride from your loving sister,
Norma

P.S. Billy was right to hand you the rose. I hope you have kept it.

*

Lucinda slips the letter inside the hidden drawer of her packing trunk, alongside the drying rosebud she has wrapped in tissue. Once they have arrived in Trenton she

[164]

will have time to re-read it; for now she tucks it away along with any thoughts of breaking up the act with Billy. It's unbearable enough as it is to think that the Hart Sisters are a thing of the past.

"You ready?" Billy pokes his head around the door. "The bellboy will be here for the trunks in a minute. I've got the train tickets," he says, patting the breast pocket of his overcoat.

"Just about." Lucinda eases the lid down and flips the latch.

"It's been quite a week, Mrs. Rogers," Billy says as he helps her into her coat.

"Hasn't it, Mr. Rogers."

Lucinda takes a furtive look at the double bed, and then at Billy, who is also looking at the bed. When he turns his gaze toward her she makes much of fiddling with the clasp of her handbag. She adjusts her hat, and takes his arm.

*

She stares out the train window at the steamships on the Hudson River and counts in her mind the number of shows remaining: two-a-day, six days at the Trent Theatre in Trenton; two-a-day, six days at the Newark Coliseum; two-a-day, six days at the new Proctor's Palace in Newark. Eighteen days, thirty-six shows.

"Whatcha' thinking about?" Billy asks, giving her a nudge with his knee, and for a moment Lucinda doesn't answer, for fear her words might catch on the small lump in her throat. Across from them sits an older couple, the severe-looking woman reading a newspaper with her eyebrows caught in a permanent frown, and the man dozing with his mouth opened beneath a carefully-waxed moustache.

"Thirty-six shows, and then it's March," Lucinda finally says, and she swallows back the lump. Billy looks at her, then out the window. The woman opposite turns the page and it gets stuck in its fold. She gives the newspaper an impatient shake, glares at her sleeping husband for a moment, and resumes reading.

"What ... I mean, what will you ..." But she can't bring herself to say the words. Billy reaches into his coat pocket as the conductor approaches, and along with the tickets he pulls out a yellow telegram and hands it to her.

DONT WORRY GOOD NEWS STOP NYC AGENT SAYS PASS-ING SHOW 1917 CASTING STOP GO SEE MAX URGENT STOP ALLS WELL TORONTO STOP MA

"I don't understand, what's the Passing Show?"

Billy looks at the telegram with a shy smile playing on his lips.

"It's a musical comedy revue at the Winter Garden The-atre. Ma thinks I should audition for it."

"The Winter Garden, isn't that Broadway?" Lucinda's eyes widen as Billy nods.

"It's a two-act revue, twenty-one scenes. Six months." Billy hands the tickets to the conductor, who punches them and hands them back.

"Six months? Billy!"

The woman across from them glances at Lucinda, her eyebrows raised in irritation.

[166]

"No-one says I've got the job, Lu. But I guess I'll go into town and see about it."

"Of course you will!" Lucinda claps her hands. "Oh, Billy, think of it!"

Billy reaches into his coat pocket again.

"There's this one, too," he says, holding out a second telegram.

POP IN MUSKOKA RELEASED GOOD BEHAVIOUR STOP MY POKER WINNINGS BOUGHT TRAIN TICKET STOP DONT WORRY ALLS WELL IN TORONTO STOP MA

"Oh my," is all Lucinda can muster. The sleeping gentleman opposite Billy utters a loud and protracted snore just as she looks at Billy from the corner of her eye, only to find him looking sideways at her. Lucinda bites her lip and stares at the floor, and the man snores again, and she can't help herself; Lucinda sneaks another look at Billy, whose shoulders are twitching. He turns toward the aisle with his hand covering his mouth, pretending to cough. Lucinda is certain the man's wife is appalled by their behaviour.

When the man utters a third, catastrophic snore, Billy stands suddenly and holds out his hand to her, all the while looking down the car as though something at the far end of it has caught his eye, but Lucinda knows from the way he is pressing his lips together that he is on the verge of a belly laugh.

She takes his hand and they hurry along the lurching car until Billy pushes the door open, and outside in the cold, on the icy platform between cars, he bursts into great, heaving gusts of laughter. Lucinda can scarcely breathe the frozen air as she gasps between guffaws of her own. She leans into him and feels the tears freezing on her cheeks and now she doesn't know whether she is laughing or crying. Billy enfolds her in his coat and they stand there together, swaying between the train cars, surrounded by occasional clouds of steam and the sound of wheels clacking their steady rhythm.

CHAPTER THIRTY-THREE

Nut & Nuttier

AT THE TRENT

The bill for the present week at the Trent Theatre opened this afternoon and on this bill are a number of acts that are sure winners and real entertainers. The bill has plenty of laughs and goes with a real snap and real vim.

The Nutt Brothers, Nutt & Nuttier, present "The Crazy Frenchman," and get all kinds of laughs. Bee-bo Gray, the king of the lariat, and Ada Sommerville, whose horse does all the latest dance steps to perfection, present a sensational Western act that is one of the outstanding big features of the bill.

Pascoe & Hart present a wonder act of ballet, song, and acrobatics. In the way of musical comedy they occupy a distinct niche of their own, graced as they are by the comedy of Mr. Pascoe and the purity of Miss Hart's soprano. Their appearance on the stage calls for repeated and long continued applause and they make a great hit.

The first number on the bill will be Nolan & Nolan, astounding jugglers who actually stop the show, and following them will be James Silver and Helen Duval in a breezy rube comedy skit entitled "Simplicity."

CHAPTER THIRTY-FOUR

Tutu

Billy leans the prop-barre pieces against the wall and hangs his coat on a hook, rubs some warmth into his hands and instantly regrets taking off his coat.

"It's worse than the coal cellar in here, I'll bet," he says.

Lucinda steps through the doorway shaking her head. She hangs up her coat, grabs her costume, and darts behind the screen.

"At least this one has a screen," Billy says, and he quickly loosens his tie and changes into his shirt, his vest, his baggy trousers. Above the mirror, the light bulb flickers, off-on-off. On again.

"I'm sure it's colder back here than it is out there," Lucinda says. "You've at least got some light."

Billy glances at the flickering bulb, the dull yellow paint on the walls. He breathes in the faintly mouldy smell so typical of the dressing rooms he's used all his life, and clips his tie in place.

"That's debatable," he says. He climbs up on his chair to tighten the bulb. "Do you need a hand?"

Lucinda holds out her blouse and skirt. "Please," she says, and as Billy takes the clothes he sees gooseflesh rising along her bare arm.

"You're turning blue with cold," he says, and he slips the blouse over a hanger. "Don't you get sick."

"Don't worry, I won't. I've been in worse dressing rooms than this."

There is a pop and a hiss, and the room falls into darkness.

"Damn," Billy mutters, and he opens the door to let in some light. "I'll go find another light bulb," he says.

"Wait, I can't see," Lucinda says. "Can you help me first? My hands are so cold, I keep dropping my sash."

She steps out from behind the screen holding her tutu in place, with the sash trailing on the floor behind her.

"I'll hold, you tie," she says.

The sash slips through his cold-stiffened fingers as Billy tries once and again to tie it, and each time it slides down her tutu to the floor.

"How about if you tie and I'll … I'll hold."

Billy takes cautious hold of the tutu, his hands practically encircling her waist while she grapples with the sash.

"Done," she says. Then she says it again. "I'm done, Billy."

The sound of men's voices erupts in the hallway as the two jugglers opening the show leave the dressing room next door and walk past. Billy lets out the breath he didn't know he was holding, and pulls his hands away as though stung.

"Would you mind handing me my shawl?"

He looks around in the half-darkness and spots it hanging over her coat. Lucinda wraps it around her shoulders and sits, shivering, on the chair by the mirror.

"How about that light bulb?" she says, and he dashes out the door to find the custodian.

*

She stands with her back to him, her head bowed and her fingers weaving in and out of each other, breathing slowly, as she always does before a performance.

"Ladies and gem'men, put your hands together for Pascoe and Hart!"

"Knock 'em dead," Billy says as she straightens and walks onto the stage, just as she has done twice a day, six days a week for the past three months. He never tires of the ritual, of watching the change in Lucinda's stance as she is flooded by the footlights. Her chin lifts slightly and her shoulders pull back as she takes her position at the barre. It's nothing the audience would notice beyond the grace of a ballerina, the confidence of a seasoned performer, but he sees the transformation in her, the strength she draws from the lights, the laughter and the applause as she moves from one world to another, from offstage to the limelight.

Together they make their way through the act, flowing seamlessly from gag to patter to song, and on to the next gag, and the audience flows with them, as much a part of the performance as Billy and Lucinda are.

As they near the end of the act and Billy goes down on bended knee, he sees that she has her hands held firmly at her waist, arms akimbo. She tries to stretch her foot, but with the awkward positioning of her arms she wobbles slightly, and puts out one hand for balance. In that instant Billy sees that her sash has come loose, and she is about to lose her tutu. Without thinking he grabs her by the waist and carries her floating to the wings, stage-right, in an unrehearsed pas de deux. He eases her to the floor and she looks at him with her mouth hanging open while her tutu drops, foaming around her ankles. Beyond the curtain the sound of laughter dwindles.

"Quick, we're losing them," he says as he grabs the tutu, trying in desperation to find the waistband in the cloud of tulle.

"Allow me." Lucinda snaps out of the shock of his lifting her, and shakes out the skirt. She pulls it up around her waist and Billy hands her the sash, which she fastens with a quick tug.

"Time, please," the stage manager calls from behind them.

"Time for a new tutu," she whispers as she rubs the boot-black around Billy's eye with one hand and smears her lip rouge with the other. Billy claps his hands and crashes to the floor, and she counts quickly to five, and strides back out into the lights. She stops midway, peeks down at her sash, smiles and shrugs at the audience, and makes her way to the wings.

CHAPTER THIRTY-FIVE

Lines

MABEL: Oh, Frederic, cannot you, in the calm excellence of your wisdom, reconcile it with your conscience to say something that will ...
(LUCINDA: Drat, I ran out of breath.
BILLY: Breathe after 'wisdom'.)
MABEL: Oh, Frederic, cannot you, in the calm excellence of your wisdom, reconcile it with your conscience to say something that will relieve my father's sorrow?
FRED: I will try, dear Mabel. But why does he sit, night after night, in this draughty old ruin?

(Billy looks up from the script he is reading, glances around the frigid dressing room, and tightens the lapels of his overcoat.)

*

MABEL: Sergeant, approach! Young Frederic was to have led you to death and glory.
(BILLY: Don't act.
LUCINDA: What do you mean by that?
BILLY: You're trying too hard. Just say it naturally.)
MABEL: Sergeant, approach! Young Frederic was to have led you to death and glory.

(LUCINDA: Better?
BILLY: Better. Don't act.)

*

FRED: ... Mabel, my dearly-loved one, I bound myself to
  serve the pirate captain until I reached my four-and-
  twenty blackbirds—
(LUCINDA: Billy!
BILLY: Sorry, I couldn't resist.)
FRED: ... until I reached my one-and-twentieth birthday.
MABEL: But you *are* twenty-one?
FRED: I've just discovered that I was born in a leap-year,
  blah-blah, and that birthday will not be reached until—
(LUCINDA: Until when?
BILLY: Are you twenty-one yet?
LUCINDA: What? Why do you ask?
BILLY: Just curious.
LUCINDA: Are you twenty-one?
BILLY: Yep, last October. But what about you?
LUCINDA: [*pauses*] I was twenty-one last Thursday.
BILLY: [*stares at her*] Last Thursday? Why didn't you say
  something?
LUCINDA: Let's keep reading. You were saying, 'blah-blah,
  and that birthday will not be reached until—'
BILLY: Last week. Your twenty-first birthday was last week.
LUCINDA: '... until 1940'. Let's read, Billy.
BILLY: Only if you promise to let me take you out to
  celebrate.
LUCINDA: Very well. I mean, thank you, I'd love to. Now,
  '... until 1940'.)

*

FRED: ... until 1940.

MABEL: Oh, horrible! Apostrophe appealing!

FRED: And so, farewell—

(BILLY: Wait a minute, that's 'Catastrophe appalling.' Ha! Good one, Lu.)

*

MABEL: Is he to die unshriven—unannealed?

(LUCINDA: I haven't the slightest idea what Mabel's talking about.

BILLY: Me neither. Just don't act.)

*

"Five minutes, Pascoe and Hart!"

"Thank you," Lucinda calls toward the door. She slips a frayed piece of ribbon trimmed from a ballet slipper between the pages and closes her script. Billy is already on his feet, pulling off his overcoat and reaching for his vest.

"Thanks for helping me with my lines, Billy. I was afraid there'd be much more than that." She takes one last look in the mirror and drapes her shawl across the chair. "Now I can concentrate on learning the music."

"Don't forget to check your sash," Billy says.

"Sorry, what?"

He points to her tutu. She tugs at the sash and smoothes the skirt. Billy holds the door open for her, and they hurry down the stairs to the wings.

*

"Thank you for a lovely meal," Lucinda says. "There's something special about an after-show dinner."

"Dinner and a show," Billy says, "Even if it's our show." He pushes the door open to the street and walks her out with his hand at her waist. "Pork chops, a baked potato, and apple pie for dessert. Nothing but the best for my girl."

"Your ... Your girl. I see."

They walk along the sidewalk with only the sound of their footsteps crunching in the snow, neither of them looking at the other.

"I've never really been anyone's 'girl' before," Lucinda finally says.

"Really? I find that hard to believe."

"It's not easy when you're on the road all the time," Lucinda says. "Besides, after our parents died, Norma was so protective of me, no-one could get near. They wouldn't dare try."

Billy throws back his head and laughs.

"I'd pity the poor fellow who'd cross Norma."

An automobile drives past slowly, leaving tire tracks in the new-fallen snow.

"My first girl was a few years older than me," Billy says. "Dora Hawthorne, a lovely little singer who was on the bill with us. I'll never forget her blonde curls, her blue eyes."

"Oh?"

"We got in a bit of trouble on our first date."

"Oh, really." A tiny frown flickers across Lucinda's brow.

"We thought we'd roast some corn, and instead we set the cornfield on fire. Our parents were furious. Ma was so angry she made me wash all the dressing room floors at the theatre every morning that week."

"Your parents … Exactly how old were you and Dora?"

"Oh, she'd have been about thirteen. I guess I was eight or nine years old."

Billy smirks and offers his arm. She takes it and gives it a squeeze.

"We've only got a few more weeks, Billy."

"I know," he says quietly, and they walk along the empty sidewalk through circles of lamplight.

*

They lie in the darkness, speaking softly, Billy on the floor and Lucinda peering over the side of the bed with her arm hanging down. They hold hands with their fingers entwined.

*

"No-one on Broadway is as funny as you are, Billy. You'll be laying them in the aisles every night."

"I need to get the job, first."

"Oh, you'll get the job. Mark my words, you'll get it."

*

"You'll be the greatest Mabel anyone's ever heard."

"I'm scared, though, Billy. As frightened as I was when you and I first broke in the act."

"There's nothing wrong with being scared. But there's a whole lot wrong with *not* being scared."

*

"What are we doing, Billy?"

"We're making sure you're not alone."

"It feels like we're playing house."

"You mean, pretending?"

"Everything's going to change soon."

"Everything's always changing, Lu."

"Let's pretend it won't. Just for now."

*

"I'll go to your opening night."

"And I'll go to yours."

"I'll send roses to your dressing room."

"And I'll send you a carnation."

"Meet me in the wings, instead."

*

Billy kisses her palm.

"Marry me, Lu."

She rests her hand on the cheekbone she blackens night after night.

"Good night, dear Billy."

CHAPTER THIRTY-SIX

Proctor's Palace, Newark, New Jersey

PROCTOR'S PALACE THEATRE
—CONTINUOUS SHOWS—

Week commencing Mon. 22 March

BILL

Davenport's Dancing Dogs
"A Wake in Hell's Kitchen"—Irish Act
Miss Ruth Gurley's Aerial Eccentricities
Mr. Julian Eltinge—Female Impersonator
Pascoe & Hart—Ballet Comedy and Song
Bedini & Arthur—The Jolly Jugglers
Belleclaire Brothers—Strong Men
AND
HELD OVER FOR A SECOND WEEK
THE GREAT LESTER—The Ventriloquist Wonder

DON ALBERT & THE PALACE ORCHESTRA
(New Show Every Monday)

CHAPTER THIRTY-SEVEN

The Palace

Billy jumps off the trolley and looks toward the theatre. A crowd has lined up along Market Street, waiting behind velvet ropes to buy tickets to the afternoon show, while ticket holders stream inside through the massive arched doors. Billy quickens his pace, keeping his head down so as not to waste time gawking at the opulent new playhouse. The Palace marquee alone is deserving of a full five minutes' attention, and he knows he could get lost in the mosaic of the lobby floor, but he is late in arriving, and Lucinda will be worried. He pulls his cap down low over his eyes and hurries past the crowds toward the stage door.

"Isn't that Billy Pascoe? Hey, Boffo Billy, over here!"

Billy glances to his left and is greeted by the sight of a skinny young man waving his hat. Beside him an even skinnier young woman has her hand on his arm, trying to shush him.

"Over here, Billy!"

He slows down slightly. If he stops moving, he'll be held up even longer.

"Enjoy the show," he calls and tips his cap, and more people in the lineup turn to look at him.

"We loved the Three Pascoes, Billy! Looking forward to seeing your new act."

"Thanks," he says, and some of the crowd begins to applaud. Billy tips his cap again and ducks around to the stage door. He hates being late, loathes drawing attention to himself before a show.

"Afternoon, Herb," he says to the security guard as he signs in.

"Good day, Mr. Pascoe. Miss Hart was asking after you."

"I'm sure she was. How is Mrs. Herb?"

"Very well, thank you. You'd better keep moving."

Billy reaches the staircase, grasps the railing and flies down six stairs at a time. By the time he reaches the dressing room, Lucinda is already dressed and made up, and is standing on one foot, holding the other foot over her head.

"There you are!" she says. "Thank goodness, I was afraid I'd have to be a single act."

"Sorry," he says. "There was a traffic accident that held the trolley up. I jumped it and ran after another one. Barely made it."

"Give me your coat, quick." Lucinda starts to unbutton his overcoat. "Well? What news?"

"I thought you'd never ask," Billy says, and he reaches inside his coat and pulls out a thick envelope. Lucinda's eyes widen as she looks first at the envelope, then at him.

"Is it the contract?" she says. "The Passing Show?"

Billy nods, and she flings her arms around him.

"Oh, Billy, you did it! I knew it, I just knew it!"

He lifts her off the ground and spins her in a circle.

"Mr. Shubert asked me if I can sing, and I said of course I can sing, and he said 'Welcome aboard,' and that was it!"

"No audition? Just like that?"

"Just like that."

"Your reputation precedes you, Boffo Billy."

Billy throws his coat across the chair and pulls off his street clothes as Lucinda hands him his costume. He is still buttoning his shirt when she begins powdering his face.

"Rehearsals start the third week in March." He spits some powder, and while Lucinda lines his eyebrows he clips his tie in place.

"That's perfect, you'll have some time to work out your act."

Billy picks up the carmine and rubs it on his lips.

"It's six months on Broadway, then we go on the road for another six. A year's work."

"A year's work, that's wonderful, Billy! Here, put on your vest."

"Shoes, where are my slap-shoes?"

"They're in your rucksack behind the chair."

"And the barre's upstairs?"

"The props manager replaced some rusted parts, and I tested it three times this morning. Don't worry, everything's ready. Here, give me your other foot."

Lucinda crouches down and laces one shoe while Billy ties the other. They finish at the same time and find themselves face-to-face.

"I'm so proud of you, Billy Pascoe." Lucinda's eyes glisten.

"Five minutes, Pascoe and Hart!"

"Ready?" she says.

He looks at her face, her blue eyes vivid against the paleness of her powder, and something deep inside of him sways and then settles.

"Ready," he says.

CHAPTER THIRTY-EIGHT

Newark Evening News

VAUDEVILLE'S LOSS IS BROADWAY'S GAIN

Today's announcement that the vaudeville sensations, Pascoe & Hart, will give their final run this week at Proctor's Palace, is sure to send a wave of sorrow through audiences not yet fortunate to have seen this corking good two-act. Anyone who has witnessed Pascoe & Hart at work on stage may be forgiven if they assume the two have performed together for years, for it is with nothing less than the finest polish and finesse that they deliver the goods. But the truth of the matter is, Billy Pascoe and Miss Lucinda Hart have shared billing but for three brief months, and they have graced enough stages on the Eastern vaudeville circuit to have amassed a fistful of solid reviews and legions of admirers.

Within weeks of each other, Mr. Pascoe and Miss Hart will each embark on new careers in show business. While Miss Hart will grace the New York Operetta Society's production of Mssrs. Gilbert and Sullivan's *Pirates of Penzance* with her ringing soprano, Mr. Pascoe, long known for headlining the rough-and-tumble comedy act the Three Pascoes, will join the cast of *The Passing Show of 1917*.

Vaudeville's loss is sure to be Broadway's gain.

Pascoe & Hart may be seen on the bill this week, Monday thru' Saturday, at Proctor's Palace, Newark, NJ.

CHAPTER THIRTY-NINE

Closing Night: Snapshots and Fragments

1. ROSES: A young woman stands with one foot on a chair, winding the ribbon from her ballet slipper around her calf. Her hair is pulled back tight, her face made up for the stage; her tutu drapes around her legs in a pale froth. On the dressing table beside her, reflected in the mirror, are a dozen roses. Unseen by the viewer: a card, written in tiny script, expressing sisterly pride and affection.

2. FIRE ESCAPE: A young man dressed in baggy trousers, vest, tie, and slap-shoes sits on the top step of a fire escape, his face lit by street lamp. A thin trail of smoke makes its way alongside him from the cigarette held between his fingers, and his gaze is pensive, his eyes hooded in the semi-darkness. Unseen by the viewer: a rusted nut concealed in the watch pocket of his vest.

3. OFFSTAGE: Two faces surrounded by dark velvet curtain, seemingly floating, lit from the stage before them. The young woman's eyes are closed and her chin slightly raised. Behind her the young man looks over her shoulder, his face alert and his mouth set, unsmiling.

4. ONSTAGE: The young man is on bended knee with one hand held out in supplication, the other hand reaching for his watch pocket. The young woman stands poised as though ready for flight. Unseen by the viewer: the flicker of confusion in the girl's eyes; a look of quiet confidence in his.

5. BOWS: The two stars stand together, holding hands and waving at the audience. They gaze up into the gallery, each of them bearing a telltale sepia smudge around their mouths. A blur of falling roses surrounds them.

*

They stand ready, one before the other. In the wings opposite and the flies above, actors and stagehands gather quietly to watch the final performance of Pascoe & Hart.

Billy places his hand on her arm, his touch soft as a shadow. For a moment Lucinda allows herself to lean against him and draw quiet strength from him.

"Ladies and gem'men ..." There is a pause and the audience quietens. "Pascoe and Hart."

The applause is deafening.

Billy breathes the words in her ear and she straightens, lifts her chin, and strides onstage. The applause continues as she takes her place at the barre. She glances at Billy, who curtsies in the wings. Taking her cue, she inclines her head toward the audience and with a shy smile, she nods her thanks.

*

They have both taken flight. Together they bring their audience to heights of laughter and heartache, and back again to joy. Billy's pratfalls are at a new level of artistry, his gags doled out effortlessly, while Lucinda plays straight as naturally as breathing. Her singing is crystalline, pure, rich with colours Billy has never heard before. Offstage and in the hall, the listeners lean forward, breathless, as she holds them in her hand with the dying notes.

> *Do you think what the end of a Perfect Day*
> *Can mean to a tired heart,*
> *When the sun goes down with a flaming ray*
> *And the dear friends have to part?*

She moves to stretch her foot, and there he is, on the wrong side. *Why is he there, he is always to her right.* He is clasping his hands to his heart, looking at her with pleading eyes.

Her only sign of confusion is a tiny crease between her eyebrows as she turns to her other foot. Impossibly, he is there waiting for her with his hands held out, palms-up. Lucinda's eyes widen as slowly he reaches with one hand for his vest pocket.

Billy tilts his head and his doe-eyes couldn't do a finer job of melting her heart. He holds before him not a ring, but a rusted nut.

"Marry him!" someone hollers from the gallery, and as Billy slips the nut on her finger, the audience erupts in applause and laughter.

Lucinda admires the rusted ring and leans over to kiss Billy's cheek. Slowly he stands, blinking at his good fortune. Lucinda grabs him by the wrist and leads him to the wings, stage right, his free hand held over his mouth as he casts a hopeful look at the audience.

*

BOWS: Sustained applause forces them back onstage again and again, urged by colleagues in the wings who whistle and clap and shout their admiration. Flowers rain down around them; Billy gives up trying to collect them all for Lucinda. When one lands at her feet, she picks it up and hands it to Billy, who, for the first time she can recall, smiles while onstage.

*

EXIT, STAGE LEFT: The stagehands and performers crowd around them, slapping Billy's back and shaking their hands. When finally there is a moment, Billy looks at Lucinda, and with words of love and thanks unspoken, they embrace in the wings.

For a long while they stand together, still and quiet, as their friends melt away behind curtains and the emcee introduces the next act.

Lucinda's makeup runs dark rivers through the snowy powder on her cheeks. Billy tightens his hold on her. The stage manager slips his hanky into Billy's hand and steps away into the darkness.

*

6. METAMORPHOSIS: The two sit side-by-side before the
   mirror, their reflected faces intent on their task. His
   sleeves are rolled up; a shawl covers her shoulders. The
   glow from the light above the mirror softens their faces
   as they wipe away the powder, the eyeliner, the lip rouge.

CHAPTER FORTY

Flickers

A young man crosses Times Square with his head down against the stinging March rain. He has spent a solitary month in the big city, eating too many pancake meals and talking to too few people. It's another world from the daily vaudeville performance routine he's lived his entire life, but now he has work to think about: soon he will appear in a Broadway touring show. There is a script to learn, gags to write.

Billy!

He hears his name being called, but ignores it. No-one knows him here; in this huge city there must be thousands of Billys.

Hey—Pascoe!

It is Lex Neal, an old friend from the vaudeville circuit. They shake hands, exchange greetings. Billy smiles a seraphic smile, happy to see a familiar face. Lex is now making moving pictures. He urges Billy to come and see what he's up to.

Flickers are the future, he says. *You interested?*

Billy's father's words come to him: *You want to show the Three Pascoes on a dirty bedsheet for a nickel a head?* he'd once said to William Randolph Hearst, insulted. But Billy is curious.

C'mon, it's Arbuckle. Come see what he's doing.

Roscoe Arbuckle, the large, genial comic whose work in *The Keystone Kops* is downright funny. The guy's a cut-up, even if he did lift one of the Pascoes' better gags. Billy hasn't anything else to do on a dreary spring day in New York City, so he follows his friend to the studio.

CHAPTER FORTY-ONE

The Butcher Boy

A young man walks into the country store, entering from the right of frame. His back faces us; he is dignified and oddly elegant in baggy overalls and slap-shoes, a flat hat perched atop his head.

Old friends stand nearby in a barrel, a cluster of brooms awaiting his magic. The young man selects one and breaks off a bristle for inspection. Not good enough. He drops the broom onto the floor and selects another. The second broom also fails inspection and he tosses it back into the barrel. With a deft kick he makes the first one somehow leap into his hand, and, looking the other way, he chucks the broom back among its comrades as though it were pulled by a magnet. But *he* is the magnet; we can't keep our eyes off him. As a five-year-old he commanded our attention onstage. Film is no different.

A molasses bucket becomes the focus of his attention. The sticky black goo is in the bucket, then it's in his hat, on his head, and now it holds his foot captive on the floor. The young man and Fatty struggle to loosen the boot. Finally Fatty gives him a hard kick to the stomach that sends him flying backward out of the store and tumbling down the steps into a spectacular pratfall.

Back inside, another big fall is to come. *Turn!* Roscoe shouts, and as the young man turns, a three-pound sack of flour hits him in the face and puts his head where his feet were. Spitting flour, he leaps up and continues with the mayhem, swinging brooms, tossing pies, dodging flour bombs and climbing the wall shelves, throwing everything within reach. It is chaos, exactly as he loves it.

His first movie shoot is done by midnight. Back at the hotel room, he can't sleep. One of Arbuckle's cameras is laid out in pieces on the bed. The young man inspects all of it, every single piece of the camera until he understands it, and then he puts it back together.

The next morning the young man quits the Broadway show, and reports to Arbuckle's studio. Roscoe looks up from his desk and says, simply, *You're late.*

You're home.

The End
&
The Beginning

Epilogue

The years have been kind to Lucinda, Billy thinks. Her eyes shine and the stage lights catch her perfectly, every angle and curve of her face, no matter which way she turns. Tonight she is the one onstage, pouring Mozart's *Queen of the Night* aria into the air, flooding the listeners' ears with the lustre and fullness of a voice more powerful in its fortieth year than it was in its twentieth.

Lucinda's high notes still reach into him, cut through the layers to his heart. Solemn-faced and breathing slowly, Billy tightens his grip on the armrests, grateful for the anonymity the darkness of the theatre brings.

He recalls the backstage-themed picture he made in the early days, the one with Arbuckle, where he thought about kissing the girl in the wings but didn't. He then thinks of his own playhouse picture, the one where he played all the instruments in the orchestra pit and all the audience members and all the singers, and he'd even danced a duet with himself. Once the dream sequence was in the can he'd shot the scene where he first kissed the wrong twin and then the right twin in the wings. After viewing the scene in the day's rushes, he'd taken the reel home where he looked at it again. Then he took up his scissors and cut it.

At the time it felt out of key with the rest of the picture, but if he were to be honest with himself, lovely as she was, the actress playing the girl simply wasn't Lu. For years Billy kept the curl of nitrate strip in a cigar box on a high shelf in his office at home, then he lost track of it, and everything else, including the home. Divorce can have that effect.

Lucinda joins the cast for her bow, and she curtsies deeply and smiles as the tenor hands her a rose. For a moment Billy closes his eyes and he is up there with her, holding her hand while the audience's love pours over them both. He can feel the heat of the spotlight, the softness of her hand, the rush of his own pulse as he catches his breath.

He could greet her at the stage door and present her with the roses he'd promised all those years ago. Instead Billy helps his fiancée with her coat and buttons up his own. He takes her by the arm and leads her through the crowd with his hat brim pulled low over his eyes. A few curious faces turn as he walks by, a small man in a frayed coat missing its top button.

Surely that's not ... Wait a minute, isn't he ... Hey, it's Billy Pascoe!

The smile on his girl's face warms him as he pushes open the glass door and they step outside into the cool evening air.

AUTHOR'S NOTE

Billy Pascoe is a character of my devising whose roots lie firmly in the early life of Buster Keaton.

Buster Keaton was born to a theatre family during vaudeville's heyday, in 1895. At nine months of age he crawled onstage with his father; at three he was a regular feature of his parents' act; and at the age of five he was on the family payroll, headlining the Three Keatons' rough-and-tumble vaudeville act. With his exceptional gifts for acrobatics and comic timing, young Buster was recognized early on as a child prodigy, and his popularity with audiences earned him the reputation as the Prince of Vaudeville.

For the first twenty-one years of his life, Buster travelled with his family all over North America, living the strenuous and nomadic life typical of vaudevillians as they moved from city to town to village, living in hotels and boarding houses. Twice a day, six days a week, the Three Keatons performed on the bill alongside a wide and eclectic range of performers.

In 1917, owing to his father's acute alcoholism, Buster broke up the family act and made his way to New York. In no time he found work with *The Passing Show of 1917*. Broadway was ready for this gifted young vaudeville star, but fate pointed him in another direction, and a chance meeting with an old friend led Buster to make a decision that would change his life, and the course of silent film comedy.

ACKNOWLEDGEMENTS

My sincere thanks to Gaspereau Press. I am deeply grateful to Sandra Barry, Mary Lou Payzant, Howard Cable, and Michelle Mulder, who read this story in its early stages. My writers' group (Carol Bruneau, Lorri Neilsen-Glenn, and Ramona Lumpkin) were the perfect midwives, involved as they were from the beginning. Avery Brennan was most helpful with his insights to the theatre; and Marina Endicott's novel, *The Little Shadows*, ignited my interest in vaudeville. Support from Patricia Eliot Tobias and the International Buster Keaton Society came at the perfect time.

I wish to thank the staff at the Margaret Herrick Library, Douglas Fairbanks Centre for Motion Picture Studies, for their patience and assistance, and for letting me hold in my hands such artifacts as Buster Keaton's datebooks and photo albums from his vaudeville years.

Among the many books I read while researching, several stand out: *Buster Keaton: My Wonderful World of Slapstick* (Buster Keaton and Charles Samuels), *Keaton* (Rudi Blesh), *Buster Keaton Interviews* (ed. Kevin W. Sweeney), *Buster Keaton Remembered* (Eleanor Keaton and Jeffrey Vance), *Writing for Vaudeville* (Brett Page), *No Applause—Just Throw Money* (Trav S.D.), and *The Complete Gilbert & Sullivan Librettos*. Original source material for the Three Pascoes reviews may be found in the *Scrapbook*, Buster Keaton Papers, Margaret Herrick Library, Academy of Motion Picture Arts and Sciences (accessed via the Margaret Herrick Library Digital Collections). The 1909 parlour songs *A Perfect Day* and *I Love You Truly* were composed by Carrie Jacobs-Bond; *Down by the Old Mill Stream* was written in 1910 by Tell Taylor.

My use of Buster Keaton as Billy's archetype was done with care and the intention of honouring his life and his art. Joe and Myra Keaton's and Roscoe Arbuckle's names I have made use of in their memory. Any historical mistakes are my own.

Thanks most especially to my children, Tamsyn and Avery, for their patience, and to Tim, always.

1   3   5   7   6   4   2

Library and Archives Canada Cataloguing in Publication

Brennan, Binnie, 1961–, author
Like any other Monday : a novel / Binnie Brennan.

ISBN 978-1-55447-138-6 (pbk.)

I. Title.

PS8603.R46IL55 2014   C813'.6   C2014-905210-3

GASPEREAU PRESS LIMITED ¶ GARY DUNFIELD
& ANDREW STEEVES ¶ PRINTERS & PUBLISHERS
47 CHURCH AVENUE KENTVILLE NS B4N 2M7
Literary Outfitters & Cultural Wilderness Guides